MISTLETOE MADNESS

A Short Story Collection

Edited by Miriam Hees
Cover Art by Elsbet Vance

Mistletoe Madness
A Short Story Collection

Blooming Tree Press
P.O. Box 140934
Austin, Texas 78714-0934

Copyright © 2004 by Miriam Hees
Cover art by Elsbet Vance
Logo by Tabi Designs
Copy editing by Peggy Brandt, Michele Chancellor
Library of Congress Catalog Card Number: 2004093501
ISBN: 0-9718348-2-2
www.bloomingtreepress.com

Printed in the United States of America

Dedication

This book is dedicated to all of those who believe in the magic of the holidays and the wonder of life.

Contents

Contents

Contents

Illustration by Terri L. Sanders

First Turkey

My name is Ginny Sue Jelks and I am in the seventh grade. Last week, I made Christmas dinner all by myself. Well, I had some help with the sides, but my job was the main course. My mamma is overseas in the army reserves. She was called up last spring and is away for a whole year. It isn't so bad having her gone. She telephones us whenever she can and e-mails us almost every week. But the special days are hard—first day of school, Thanksgiving, and especially my birthday. Those are the days when a kid really needs her mom.

Each year, we host the big Christmas dinner and Mamma makes the turkey. Since Mamma's not around, Auntie Dee volunteered to have Christmas at her house, but I said "No way. We're not breaking with tradition. I'll make the turkey." I half-hoped that Dad would jump in to stop me, but he just looked at me with prideful eyes.

"Look at Ginny, already twelve years old and going to make her first turkey."

Sometimes my mouth gets ahead of me, so when Auntie Dee offered to help, I said "Thanks, but I've cooked with Mamma plenty of times, and I'm ready to do it myself." Everyone nodded and smiled while my insides crumbled. What had I volunteered to do? Could I really cook a turkey without Mamma?

My brother, Will, should have been the one to shoulder the turkey responsibility, seeing as he's two years older. But he recently decided to become a vegetarian. He might have offered to make a tofu-loaf or something, which would send Grandpa over the edge. If there's one thing my Grandpa likes, it's meat. So it was up to me to save Grandpa and save the dinner.

* * * *

Mamma e-mailed me two weeks before Christmas:

Hi Honey,
Dad told me that you're hosting the big dinner.

2

MISTLETOE MADNESS

What a grown-up thing to do! If you look in the kitchen cabinet you'll find my recipes. Let me know if you have any trouble. I love you and miss you.
Love,
Your Mamma
P.S. Don't forget to defrost the turkey.

I found my mamma's recipe for roasted turkey in her recipe files. It looked simple enough. Basically, you pop it in the oven for a few hours. The hardest part was determining what size turkey to get. Mamma's card said to plan on one and a half pounds per adult. There would be six turkey-eating adults, (I counted myself as an adult; I was, after all, the cook) and two little kids, so I decided that ten pounds would be about right. I told Dad to bring home one ten-pound bird, which we put directly into the freezer.

* * * *

The week before Christmas, the menu was planned. Dad would make his clam dip and Will would make a salad. The relatives would bring the rest. All I had to do was roast the turkey and make the stuffing. Stuffing was a controversial issue in our family. Mamma liked to put it in the turkey to bake but Will complained that she

3

MISTLETOE MADNESS

was inviting bacteria to come to dinner. Since bacteria make me nervous, I opted to bake the stuffing separately.

That night I got another e-mail from Mamma:

Hi Honey,

It sounds like you've got the whole dinner organized. You may want to buy an extra can of olives for your cousins. I wish that I could be there to help you, but I know you'll do great! I love you and miss you.

Love,

Your Mamma

P.S. Did I remind you to defrost the turkey?

* * * *

Christmas Eve was full of last minute details. I wrapped presents, hung the fancy towels in the bathroom, and decorated the house with sprigs of mistletoe. I made the stuffing ahead of time and tucked it safely in its own dish. All I'd need to do tomorrow was bake it while the turkey was cooking.

We were all missing Mamma that night. We went to church early and then went to the movies. It was nice to eat popcorn and not worry about the dinner, or wonder what was happening thousands of miles away. When we got home, I went right to sleep.

4

MISTLETOE MADNESS

Now, I don't care if I am practically a teenager. I know that I'm supposed to be of an age where I sleep until noon, like Will, but I am an early bird. So that morning I woke up with the sun and ran out to the living room. Dad gave me a hug and said "Merry Christmas, Ginny." He handed me a mug of hot cocoa. Then, lo and behold, who should come strolling down the hall, but Will. "Why son, what a surprise to see you up so soon. Merry Christmas." Will returned Dad's hug and stumbled to the couch.

Dad made more cocoa and we exchanged gifts. I gave Dad a sweater and Will an alarm clock. I opened a new dictionary from Will. He explained, "It's the pocket kind, so you can carry it with you to the library and stuff."

"Thanks, Will." I didn't ask him why I'd need my own dictionary at the library. When your big brother does something nice, you just say thank you and don't ask too many questions. Otherwise, he might get his feelings hurt and take it back.

Dad handed me a small box. "It's from your mom and me." I carefully unwrapped the paper and opened the box. Inside was a silver pen with my name engraved in gold:Ginny Sue Jelks.

"Oh, Daddy, it's beautiful!" I hugged him.

MISTLETOE MADNESS

The phone rang and Dad answered, "Happy holidays."

It was Mamma! First Dad talked, and then Will mumbled a few words to her. Finally, it was my turn. I carried the phone to the kitchen, for privacy.

"Merry Christmas, Ginny! How is your morning going?" I told her about how pretty the house was and thanked her for the pen. "Darling that's wonderful. I wish I could see everything. I can't wait to hear how the dinner turns out. Did you defrost the turkey?" Uh-oh. My heart sank as I realized that I'd forgotten that one little detail. But before I could confess my mistake, she said, "Honey, I've got to run. I'll call you soon. Love you." And she was gone. I was all alone.

I rushed to pull the turkey out of the freezer. It was a solid block of ice. On the label it said, "Allow at least one day of thawing for every four pounds of turkey." With a ten-pound turkey I should have taken it out three days ago! It was already ten o'clock. Dinner was supposed to be in seven hours. My eyes burned, but I didn't have time to cry. I quickly dialed the toll-free number on the turkey package.

"Plump 'N Juicy Turkey, this is Granny Bess.

How can I help you?"

"Oh Ma'am, I'm in a huge mess. The turkey—it's frozen. I never took it out and everyone' coming and my Mamma's not here. I thought I could cook it myself, but now I need help!"

She chuckled and said, "Now don't you worry, pumpkin, I'll tell you how to do the quick defrost method." She told me to soak the turkey in cold water. In a few hours, the turkey would be ready to roast. There was nothing else to do but turn on the tap and fill the sink.

Every thirty minutes I added fresh water. When Dad asked how the turkey was coming, I bit my lip and answered, "Fine, just fine." Mamma always said that a watched pot never boils. Well I'm here to attest that a watched turkey never thaws. It took five hours before that bird was ready and then I had to wash it and take all of the yucky parts out. Dinner was going to be late. Really late.

By four o'clock, the turkey was in the oven at last, and the family began to arrive. Aunt Sally and Uncle Pete came with the cousins, Clara and Owen. Uncle Pete set the pies in the kitchen. "Sure smells good in here, Ginny. I can't wait to eat.

"Thanks. Can I offer you some dip?" I held the

bowl and a plate of crackers. The doorbell rang. It was Auntie Dee and Grandpa.

"Hi, sugar. Let me plug this in." Auntie Dee set up her slow cooker filled with mashed potatoes. "They should stay warm for an hour or so." Try four hours, I wanted to say. Grandpa handed me his infamous sweet potato casserole.

"Now, put this in the oven so the marshmallows get nice and crispy."

"Sure, I'll put it in soon," I lied. I couldn't bear to confess that dinner was still a long way off. So I decided to stall. "Dip anyone?" We moved to the living room and talked until the dip ran out. It was almost five o'clock, but nobody noticed. "Let me go get some more snacks." Everyone kept talking while I rummaged through the refrigerator. I found a bag of baby carrots and dumped them in a bowl.

I passed the bowl around. Aunt Sally told the kids to wash for dinner. "No! Not yet!" I shouted. I ran to the closet and pulled out a game. "Let's play Monopoly, first!" Everyone stared at me as if I'd grown horns. Nobody said a word. After a minute or two, Will broke the silence, "Okay. I'll be the race car." I was so grateful, I could have hugged him.

We'd played half a game before Cousin Clara whined, "I'm hungry. When's dinner?" I looked at the clock. We still had over an hour to go. Then I remembered the olives. Oh, thank you Mamma! I dashed to the kitchen and poured them in a bowl.

"For you, from Mamma," I said as I handed them over to the kids, who promptly stuck olives on each finger. The grown-ups resumed playing.

Then something horrible happened.

Grandpa won the game. He had a string of luck and bought all of the properties, and I wallowed in bankruptcy. Just like that. Dad said, "Now, let's eat!" Everyone jumped up. Will tossed his salad and Auntie Dee heated the sweet potatoes; Grandpa and Uncle Pete set the table. Aunt Sally helped the kids put out the water glasses. Dad pulled the turkey out of the oven to cool. I should have stopped them, but I couldn't open my mouth to protest. I simply stood there. Frozen.

Everyone sat at the table. I waited. I imagined what was going to happen. My first Christmas dinner and I was serving a raw bird. We would all die from the deadly bacteria of uncooked poultry. I wondered who would be the one to find us. Maybe I should unlock the door for the coroner.

It must have been a miracle. Not the kind of biblical proportion, but the small kind of miracle that you read about in the Digest. Before Dad carved the bird, he checked the thermometer. "Perfect," he said. Now I know that there was no way on earth that turkey had time to cook through. But I swear he sliced that turkey and it was completely cooked. He passed the platter around and everyone "oohed" and "aahed." I watched while Grandpa took a bite. He smiled at me. Dad took a taste. "My compliments to the chef." My hand shook as I tried a piece. It melted in my mouth. It was absolutely delicious. I nearly wept with relief.

We dug in. All of the food was superb and I was ravenous. We polished off the entire meal, even Grandpa's sweet potatoes. I wished Mamma could have been there. She would have loved it. I sat tall and knew that I'd done a good job, even though I needed a little help.

* * * *

That night, after the relatives went home, I checked my e-mail. There was a message:

10

MISTLETOE MADNESS

Hi Honey,
Sorry that I couldn't talk longer this morning. I wish that I could have been there to help you today. You were so courageous to tackle a big dinner like this. I love you and miss you.
Love,
Your Very Proud Mamma
P.S. Your dinner was perfect. Well done, darling.

I couldn't figure out how she knew that the dinner was a success, but she did. Must be a Mamma-thing.

Anyway, I was exhausted and climbed into bed. It had been a long day, and I needed some sweet dreams.

Next year, maybe we'll order pizza.

Cassandra Reigel Whetstone

Christmas Eve Wishes

Our gifts are stacked and laced
With ribbons curling bright
For every child who's yearning
I wish a gift tonight.

Our dinner plates sparkle
On the tablecloth white
I wish all hungry families
Will have a feast tonight.

As carols play softly
Our Christmas tree's alight
I wish a peaceful evening
For the whole wide world tonight.

Mary Cronin

MISTLETOE MADNESS

Illustration by Agy Wilson

The Christmas Candle

Anna licked her lips and stared at the crusty loaf of bread. It was all her family had to eat.

Tomorrow, she would hear church bells ring in Christmas across the valley, like angel songs in the crisp air. What would they eat then?

Anna looked out the window. Flakes of snow glittered in the faint light. Anna watched Papa place a candle in the window and light it with a glowing twig.

"Papa, that is our last candle," Anna protested.

Papa settled her on a tattered rug by the fire. "Every house in the village lights a Christmas candle. How else could a lost traveler find shelter?"

MISTLETOE MADNESS

A blast of wind shuddered against the walls outside. Anna stared at the flames dancing in the fireplace, then at the tiny light in the window.

"I don't think the candle helps at all," she said. "We should blow it out."

Anna's stomach was hollow and hard. She licked her lips as the candle burned. The door rattled suddenly.

"Help us, help us," a man's voice begged.

Anna stood up, afraid.

Papa spread his arms wide. "Welcome, strangers."

He led the strangers to the fire. Drops of ice melting off their clothes sizzled on the ashes, and a baby in the woman's arms shivered with cold.

"You must be hungry," Mama said as she took their coats away.

Anna's heart froze.

"Anna, slice the bread and bring it in to us," Papa said cheerfully. "It is too cold to eat in the kitchen."

Anna trudged away, tears stinging against her eyes.

"I've been hungry all day," she muttered, "and it's our food."

MISTLETOE MADNESS

She stood on a chair and sliced the bread with short, angry strokes. She reached the center where the bread was dense and smelled of yeast and butter. Anna hesitated.

She began to cut a thin slice, then moved the knife further back and cut it thick and fat. She slipped the piece of bread into her apron pocket, then piled the other slices upon a plate.

She tiptoed to the chest against the wall and opened the bottom drawer. She lifted a dress and some underclothes. She touched Grandma's silky handkerchief from better days, when there had been work in the mountains. Anna hid the slice of bread under the handkerchief.

"Anna?"

"I'm coming," she called.

Her mother brought in a jug of goat's milk from outside where it was cooling. Anna handed her the plate of bread and filled three mugs. When the visitors finished drinking, Anna's family would use the mugs.

Anna's stomach rumbled. *Hurry, she thought. I can't wait.*

MISTLETOE MADNESS

The woman dunked bread into the baby's cup of milk and fed it to him. The baby sighed and mushed the bread and opened his little pink mouth again and again. Finally, the strangers were done. Anna took two slices of bread and stuffed half of one into her mouth. The baby watched her chew.

"We would have frozen if we hadn't seen your candle," the man and woman told Anna's parents.

The baby fell asleep under a ragged blanket. Later, Papa poked the fire and added a huge chunk of wood. "Time for bed," he told Anna. "Tomorrow we will hear the Christmas bells."

The woman crept close to her baby. Firelight settled across her arms like shredded rags of gold and ruby.

"Thank you for your kindness," she said.

Anna wrapped her blanket around her shoulders. She thought of the bread she had hidden, and her heart felt like a stone in her chest.

"It was just a small slice," she told herself. "Not enough for anyone but me."

Anna fell asleep. Then she heard a dreadful sound. "Oh!" Anna cried, and put her hands over her ears. Still, she heard the sound.

Anna crept close to the fire, where the woman rocked her baby.

"Why won't he be quiet?" Anna asked.

The woman's face glistened with tears.

"He's hungry," she said.

"But he ate his supper."

The woman shook her head sadly. "He is small, and grows so fast." She pulled a piece of bread from her pocket. "I saved half of my own portion, to feed him tomorrow."

Anna looked at the woman's slice of bread. Had she really cut them all so small?

The baby continued to wail. Tears rolled down his cheeks.

"Times are hard," Anna said.

The baby grasped her thumb with a tight, hard fist. His fingers were like soft pink flowers in springtime. He began to sob again, and Anna's lips trembled.

She slid away from the fire and tiptoed to the chest of drawers in the kitchen. Slowly, she lifted the silken square and took out the piece of bread.

"It is such a little slice," she whispered. "Better for a small tummy." She tucked the handkerchief into her pocket and ran back to the fire.

"Here," she said. "Give him this."

She poured the last bit of milk from the jug next to the door.

"Here," she said again.

The woman nodded and took the mug. She dipped small chunks of bread into the rich milk.

"I'm grateful," she whispered. "You have given me your treasure."

Anna took her silken handkerchief and warmed it before the fire. She gently smoothed away the tears drying on the baby's cheeks . . . one, two, three, four. A tear in the corner of his right eye squeezed out and rolled away, and Anna caught it in the handkerchief. Five.

"You can have this, too," she told the woman.

"Oh, no. You have your own tears to wipe away," the woman replied.

She smiled. "I will kiss away my baby's tears."

19

MISTLETOE MADNESS

Anna watched the baby eat and stretch and squirm in his mother's arms. Then she closed her eyes and pulled her blanket over her shoulders. "I want to hear the angel songs in the morning," she muttered, and fell asleep.

Ring a ding! Ring ling, ring ling!

"Anna, wake up! Listen!"

Mama opened the door and Anna snuggled into her father's arms as the Christmas bells sang into the crisp winter morning.

"Where are the strangers from last night?" Anna asked.

"Gone," said Papa. "They needed to be home on Christmas Day."

He shut the door. "The air is like ice," he told them, "but I must gather wood."

Anna reached into her pocket. "Wait, Papa! You can tie Grandma's handkerchief over your face to keep out the wind."

She pulled out the silk handkerchief.

"Mama! Papa!" she shrieked.

Her parents stared. Anna pointed to the glistening drops upon the cloth. One, two, three, four, five.

"What?" The three looked down in wonder.

MISTLETOE MADNESS

Five diamonds, hard and pure, flashed in the sunlight. Anna looked out the window again, and heard the angel songs ringing across the valley. Her heart felt wide and open.

"Why did they give me such a treasure?" Anna wondered. She gulped and picked at a speck of brown that lay against the bright diamond.

Then she saw what it was—such a silly thing to be caught in the same handkerchief as the diamonds.

It was only a bread crumb.

Carla Joinson

Christmas in a Pickle Jar

Mitchell gazed out the window of Grandma's big farm kitchen. Large snowflakes filled the frame as they floated to the ground.

Grandma opened the door of the cast-iron stove and checked the roasting turkey. A wisp of gray hair escaped her bun and she smoothed it back into place with one hand. "A bit longer yet," she said, poking the bird with a fork. "I think I'll add more wood to keep the temperature up." She lifted the lid to the firebox and added a few pieces.

Mitchell jumped from his chair. "Can I get more wood for the stove?"

"No, thank you. Grandpa brought in enough after

milking the cows," Grandma said.

Mother hummed a Christmas carol while she peeled carrots.

"Can I do that?" Mitchell asked.

Mother shook her head. "No, you might cut yourself."

Mitchell ran to the sink. "Can I pump more water for you?"

Mother shook her head. "No, what you can do is stay out of the way."

Mitchell slumped. "Why can't I help?"

"I guess we're used to doing it ourselves," Grandma said, wiping her hands on her apron.

"Why don't you go play?" Mother asked.

Mitchell put his thumbs in his suspenders and rocked on his heels. "I want to go sledding."

"Mitchell, it is too cold for you to go sledding. If this storm keeps up, you may have to wait until we return to the city."

"But Grandpa made me a new sled and there's a great hill just past the trees. Just once, please?"

Mother stopped peeling and stared at him. The look in her eyes told him the answer before she spoke.

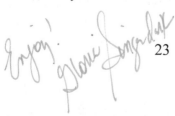

MISTLETOE MADNESS

"No."

Mitchell sighed and leaned against the doorframe. A gust of wind blew in under the front door and up the back of his wool blazer. Mitchell shivered and stepped closer to the stove. Grandma turned to put a bowl of pickles on the table and bumped into him. The pickles bounced in the bowl and almost spilled onto the floor.

"Mitchell, can't you find *something* to do?" Mother asked.

"No," he said with a shrug.

"Well, let's see if *I* can find something for you then," said Grandma. She washed the empty pickle jar, pulled a glass jug from the pantry and pulled off its cloth cover.

"What's that?" asked Mitchell.

"Settled cream," said Grandma.

She poured some of the cream into the jar, placed the lid back on tight and handed it to Mitchell. "Now, go sit in the front room with your father and Grandpa. Shake that as hard as you can and watch what happens. When the cream sounds watery, bring it here."

Mitchell shuffled down the hall. He shook the jar as Grandma had asked, up and down, back and forth.

Nothing seemed to happen.

After a while, though, the sound did change. It didn't sound as thick anymore. Mitchell peered into the jar. Resting on the bottom was a small, white lump. He shook the jar even harder, over his head, from side to side and tucked in close to his belly—up and down. Soon the lump had grown and the liquid around it sounded just like water. He raced to the kitchen.

"Look! There's something in the jar!" he exclaimed.

"Yes, Mitchell, now let's see what you've made." Grandma poured the liquid from the jar through a mesh sieve into a mixing bowl. Left in the sieve was a white nugget.

"What's that?" Mitchell asked.

Mother smiled. "Butter."

"But butter comes from the store and besides, it's supposed to be yellow," Mitchell said.

"Not fresh farm-made butter," said Grandma. "Now what we have left in the bowl is buttermilk. I think we'll make hotcakes for breakfast in the morning." Grandma put the bowl into the icebox. "Now run and get your father and Grandpa for dinner."

MISTLETOE MADNESS

Everyone sat around the table. The turkey was carved and their plates were filled with food.

"Thank you for preparing such a wonderful meal," Grandpa said. "And Mitchell, thank you for making such fine butter."

Mitchell smiled. "I'm just glad I could help."

Gloria Singendonk

How to Make Unsalted Butter

You will need:
Jar with tight-fitting lid
Whipping Cream, without stabilizer (fresh)
Mesh Sieve

1. Fill a jar 2/3 full with whipping cream.
2. Shake for 20 minutes or until butter forms and liquid sounds thin like water.
3. Pour over a sieve and discard liquid or use in your favorite buttermilk recipe.
4. Place butter on a dish and serve.

A Gift for Zane

Emily leaned against the rail fence and shivered. Only a few weeks before, the leaves on the trees had been as bright as her own coppery-orange hair, but now they lay brown and mucky on the ground, as dismal as the gray skies and the stark trees.

"I hate November," Emily muttered to Agatha. Agatha only nodded and huddled deeper into her coat. As usual, their class had gotten out first, something they lorded over the others when the weather was fine. In weather like this, however, waiting wasn't fun.

Finally Harry straggled out, followed by Billy, and then Jared. Emily could see her cousins' breath form white clouds in the air as they crossed the schoolyard. A

27

minute later, her older sister, Dorthea, was also hurrying towards them.

"Aren't we waiting for Zane?" Emily asked as they headed for home, their feet squelching wetly against the old leaves.

"He had detention," Dorthea said.

"How come?"

"Mr. Hardy blamed him for putting a dead mouse in Lila Crawford's desk."

Emily bristled. "Zane wouldn't do that!"

"Tom Watson did it," Dorthea said matter-of-factly. "But Mr. Hardy doesn't know that, and Zane didn't tell him. You know how Zane is."

Yes, she knew how Zane was. He was angry and quiet and he never seemed to care what other people thought of him. Since the day he and his crotchety old father had moved into the rundown squatter's shack bordering her family's orchard two years ago, Zane had been a mystery to her. Emily had liked him immediately because he always listened to her and never treated her like a silly little girl, even if he was three years older. Still, there was no denying that he was peculiar, and though he wasn't the type of boy who put mice in people's desks, he could be downright rude to Jared and Billy and her older brother, Brett. None of them really liked Zane's company, except Emily, and even she got the feeling that Zane merely put up with her and didn't really consider her a friend.

"Zane's dumb," Billy said. "You wouldn't catch me taking the blame for something somebody else did, 'specially so close to Christmas."

Jared rolled his eyes at his younger brother. "Christmas? It's not even Thanksgiving yet."

"You can never be too careful," Billy said wisely.

Emily gave her cousin a poke. At eight, he was a year younger than she was, but acted like a know-it-all. She enjoyed teasing him whenever she could. "You think Santa'll knock you off his list if you misbehave?"

"Santa's for babies like Harry here," Billy said scornfully, giving his little brother a shove. "But if you get in enough trouble, your parents give you less presents. Mama's threatening already."

Jared shook his head. "She doesn't mean it."

"You can never be too careful," Billy repeated.

Emily thought of the pile of tissue paper-wrapped gifts under her own bed. It might not be Thanksgiving yet, but she was never one to put things off. She'd bought all her gifts at the dime store in Danville last Saturday, spending the dollar Dad had given her for helping with the apple harvest plus an extra seventy-five cents carefully extracted from her coffee-tin bank. She felt proud of herself, spending only $1.75 when she had so many people to buy for—Mama and Dad and Brett and Dorthea, Uncle Ernest and Aunt Maude and the four cousins, Agatha and Agatha's mother and aunt, and Miss Marshall, the best fourth grade teacher there ever was.

She'd spent an hour walking up and down between the counters at the dime store, making her purchases carefully, trying to imagine what people would buy for themselves if money wasn't so tight. Mama said the Depression meant people had to be practical, but Emily didn't think Christmas and practical went together, and she bought mostly wish-gifts, things people wished for but never bought for themselves. She was highly satisfied with all her purchases, particularly the little mirror she'd gotten for Agatha that looked almost like the kind grown-up ladies carried in their purses, and the palm-sized doll with the happy grin she'd bought for her four-year-old cousin Elenor. She wished for both gifts herself, and while she'd hinted about the mirror to Mama, she hadn't mentioned the doll. She knew nine years old was too old for dolls.

Even with all those gifts safely under her bed, Emily felt a little uneasy. She hadn't gotten a gift for Zane. He was her neighbor, just like Agatha, and really that was as good as family. Yet Emily knew that Zane was different than her siblings and cousins and Agatha. He was always outside their friendly group by his own choice, not theirs. It was hard to be friendly with Zane, but she still wanted to give him a Christmas present.

Emily turned to Jared, who always gave good advice. "D'you think I should get Zane a Christmas gift?"

Billy answered first. "Zane? What would you do a silly thing like that for?"

"I wasn't asking you," she told him, wondering if it was too late to return a certain neatly wrapped yo-yo that was under her bed.

She turned back to Jared. He was always more polite than Billy, but his eyebrows were raised. "I wouldn't, Em," he said slowly. "You know how Zane is. Likely he'd think it was charity and throw it right back in your face."

31

"He's my friend," she said, jutting out her chin.

"Suit yourself. He won't like it, though."

"He'll hate it!" Billy crowed, kicking at a pile of rotting leaves.

They had reached the orchard that Emily's father and uncle owned and, in the distance, she could see the ramshackle cabin where Zane and his father lived. It matched the weather in its dreariness. How could Zane stand to live there? Billy made it sound as though Zane didn't have any feelings, but Emily knew he did. He deserved a Christmas gift just like everyone else. Even though she usually trusted Jared's advice absolutely, this time she just couldn't agree with him.

* * *

Her problem, she finally decided, was that she didn't know what to get him. She figured that boys that age were just hard to find presents for, but then she remembered that she'd had no trouble finding gifts for Jared (a mystery book) and Brett (a fancy pen to write his high school compositions with). She admitted to herself that it was just Zane who was difficult to shop for.

After a week of thinking, Emily turned to her sister Dorthea for help. After all, Dorthea was twelve, the same age as Zane, and she tended to know things Emily didn't.

"You're really going to get a present for Zane?" Dorthea asked when Emily told her. From the tone of her voice, you would have thought Emily had suggested buying a gift for one of the apple trees.

Emily ignored the tone. "Yes, but I don't know what to get him."

Dorthea twirled one of her brown curls, deep in thought. "What he *needs* are some new clothes. Warmer ones, too. But of course you can't get him that."

Emily nodded. Even if she could afford clothes, which she couldn't, she could picture Zane throwing them back at her just as Jared had predicted.

"Maybe you ought to try to ask him what he wants," Dorthea suggested. "Not outright, mind you, but just sort of hint around."

Emily knew she wasn't as good at hinting around as Dorthea was, but she decided to give it a try. She waited for Zane one afternoon, putting up with the raw weather so she could walk home from school with him. He'd had detention again and was in no mood to talk.

"Why'd Mr. Hardy keep you after this time?" she

asked.

He didn't answer right away, but she knew enough to be patient and after awhile he said, "Thought it was me who hid his chalk."

"Was it?"

"No."

"Did you tell him that?"

Zane looked sideways at her with his stormy blue-gray eyes. "He didn't ask."

"Zane!" she cried. "You oughta speak up for yourself!"

He shook his head. "It doesn't matter, not with this. I don't care a lick what Mr. Hardy thinks of me."

She tried to change the subject. "Christmas is coming."

"So?"

"So aren't you excited?"

He looked at her like she was crazy. "What's there to be excited about? 'S just a day like any other."

His words hit her like concentrated sadness, and she could hardly say good-bye to him when he turned off towards the rickety little house. Imagine saying Christmas was like any other day!

MISTLETOE MADNESS

She continued trying to think of what to get him on her own, and in the meantime she helped Mama with plans for Christmas dinner. Uncle Ernest and Aunt Maude were coming, and the cousins, of course, and Agatha and her mother and aunt. As Mama tried to figure out how much food they'd need, Emily asked, "Can we invite Zane, too?"

Mama looked at her. "If we invited Zane, we'd have to invite his father."

"Well, can we?" Emily asked, even though she knew Mama would refuse. Everyone thought Zane was an enigma, but they downright disliked his blunt, scruffy-looking father.

Mama surprised her. "You can invite them if you want," she said, and Emily smiled for a moment before Mama added, "I doubt they'll say yes."

Emily spent two days trying to figure out who she should pose the invitation to, Zane or his father, and decided they were both equally likely to refuse it. In the end, she decided to ask both of them together. Screwing up her courage (for she was secretly a little afraid of Zane's father), she walked to their gate one day after school.

MISTLETOE MADNESS

Father and son were in the yard breaking up kindling; they were the only people Emily knew who still used a wood-burning stove. They stopped when they saw her, but neither said hello.

"I-I came to invite you to Christmas dinner," Emily said, aware that she was mumbling. She wished she could scamper out of the yard like a squirrel. What had possessed her to ask them, anyway?

Zane frowned at a pile of branches. His father looked at Emily and narrowed his eyes a little. "How come?"

"W-what?" she stammered.

"How come you're asking us?"

"Because you're our neighbors. And I'd like you to come."

He continued to stare her down. He was an older man and not very tall, but he seemed large and powerful to Emily. When he spoke, his voice split the crisp, dry air. "I think you're lying, girl. You don't care a bit whether I'm at your Christmas dinner or not."

Emily cringed at the accusation, but fear quickly turned to anger. She jutted out her chin and looked the old man in the eyes. "You're right. I don't care one bit if you're there or not. But Zane's my friend and I want him to come, and I had to be polite and ask the both of you."

She was horrified as soon as the words were out of her mouth. She could imagine what Mama would say about her manners, if she only knew. But to her surprise, Zane's father was laughing, a raspy cackle that sounded amused, if not happy. "Good for you, girly! Good for you! You told me," he said. "All right, then. We'll be at your Christmas dinner."

"Good," Emily murmured, and made her escape. She was aware that Zane hadn't once looked up, or said a word.

* * *

Mama said several times in the first weeks of December that homemade gifts were the best. Emily knew this was meant to be a hint so that she wouldn't be disappointed on Christmas when the gifts she received weren't store bought, but she took the advice to heart and decided to knit a scarf for Zane.

Even with this plan, she didn't feel overly confident. Dorthea could knit wonderfully, but her own needles always wobbled and, in truth, a scarf was the only thing she *could* knit. It seemed like a pathetic gift, and she wouldn't blame Zane for scorning it, even though he could use it.

She set to work, choosing the brightest red yarn on a whim and then regretting it later. Everything about Zane was so dark and somber. She should have chosen brown or gray.

She knit on doggedly, and had Dorthea help her make a fringe at both ends. She wrapped it up in tissue paper and put it under her bed with the rest of her gifts, glad when its gaudiness was out of sight.

The whirlwind of Christmas swept her into its merriment. She made paper chains with her little cousins, Harry and Elenor, and refused to get angry when Billy teased her about it. She baked cookies with Mama and Dorthea, went with Dad and Brett to find a tree, and made new tin foil wings for the angel all by herself. She hardly thought of Zane, and he hadn't said ten words to her since the invitation. Normally she would have been fed up with him, but Christmas had her too excited to care.

Christmas day dawned with the sun making sparklers on the two-day-old snow outside. The presents looked so beautiful under the tree that Emily almost hated to open them. But of course she did, curling up next to

MISTLETOE MADNESS

Dad on the rug while Brett played Santa and doled out the gifts. She got more than she had expected, and not all of them were homemade or useful, either, including a little mirror every bit as nice as the one she'd gotten Agatha, and the newest Lucy Maud Montgomery book that she'd been longing to read. There was a new winter coat, too, in such a pretty shade of blue that she counted it as a good gift rather than a useful one.

They ate breakfast, and then Uncle Ernest and Aunt Maude and the cousins arrived and there were more gifts to be opened. The room seemed to be bursting with light and happiness and the delicious smells that were beginning to waft in from the kitchen. Emily hardly noticed that Agatha and her family had arrived until her friend grabbed her in a Christmas hug.

"Merry Christmas, Emily!" Agatha spun around like a ballerina so that the skirt of her plaid dress flared out. "Isn't it beautiful? Mama worked on it all month and I never knew about it 'til today."

"It's gorgeous," Emily agreed.

They exchanged gifts, and Emily assured Agatha that she loved her new cross-stitched bookmark. Maybe Mama was right about homemade gifts being best after

39

all.

Zane and his father didn't arrive until just before dinner. Both of them looked different. The old man's grizzled beard was trimmed, and he wore a musty but well-cut suit. He gave Emily's mother a sprig of holly with a gruff, "Merry Christmas." Zane's black hair was slicked down for once and he was wearing a tie with his usual frayed but clean shirt. He looked only slightly miserable.

There was no time to give him his present before dinner. They sat down to eat, and between bites of ham, mashed potatoes, applesauce, carrots, and biscuits, Emily managed to notice that Zane looked somewhat happier. She guessed he didn't often have meals like this.

After the dinner plates were cleared away, dessert was served: pumpkin pie, apple pie, chocolate layer cake, and four kinds of Christmas cookies. Emily nibbled at a piece of cake and wished she hadn't eaten so much dinner. She marveled at how Brett and Jared could devour a slice of everything as though they hadn't eaten in days. And look at Zane! He matched them slice for slice, and when Mama asked him if he'd like another piece of cake he held out his plate and said, "Yes, ma'am," and smiled like a little boy. Somehow, that smile made Emily feel warm inside.

When everyone had eaten their fill, even the boys, Dorthea and Emily helped Mama and Aunt Maude clear the table and wash the dishes. Even a mundane chore like that seemed more special on Christmas. Aunt Maude started singing carols, and they brought the songs with them into the living room when the dishes were done. Agatha's mother sat at the piano and played for them, and they sang through all the familiar carols and hymns. Emily could feel the happiness pulsing through every song.

When they finished singing together, Aunt Maude sang "Silent Night" by herself, her silvery voice soaring like a Christmas dove. After that, Emily sang a duet of "O Holy Night" with Agatha, and then Dorthea said she wanted to sing "Carol of the Bells," but she needed a tenor to harmonize with.

The men in the family looked at one another; none of them could carry a tune.

"Fine, then," Dorthea sighed. "I'll sing alone."

Before Agatha's mother could begin to play, however, a voice growled, "You, boy. Sing for them."

They all turned to look at Zane's father, sitting in

the shadows of the corner, and then at Zane, whose face was turning red. Emily felt sure he'd refuse, but when Dorthea said beseechingly, "Oh, do, Zane," he nodded and got up to stand beside the piano.

The song was such a pretty one, and Emily hugged herself against the warmth of it. She knew her sister sang beautifully, but to her surprise Zane did, too. It was the happiest she'd ever heard him sound, and his voice blended into one with Dorthea's, winding a trail of music around the room that glowed brighter than any candle. The song ended all too soon, with Zane hurriedly sitting down, face flushed. A hush fell over the room for a moment, and Emily knew everyone had appreciated the song as much as she had.

She waited until the others had started to sing again before scooting over beside Zane and passing him the present. "It's not much," she said miserably.

He reached into his pocket and handed her something lumpily wrapped in newspaper. "Neither is mine," he muttered.

She looked at him, shocked that he was giving her a present.

"Go on, open it," he all but growled.

42

She unwound the grimy paper to reveal a tiny doll similar to the ones at the dime store, only carved out of wood. She stared at it in disbelief.

"I know it isn't much," Zane said. "Just something I made . . ."

"I love it," she said honestly, looking him straight in the eyes, hoping he knew she meant it. "It's just what I wanted."

He shrugged and began to open his own present. Emily felt her face grow hot. The scarf seemed even more pathetic than before, not the right gift at all.

Zane held it in his hands, running a calloused finger over the bright red wool. "You made this yourself?"

She nodded. "I'm sorry I didn't get you something better . . ."

He looked at her, puzzled. "Nah, this is just right." He flung the scarf around his shoulders and gave her a half smile. But his face grew serious again as he said, "Thank you, Emily."

He sounded so sincere, so unlike Zane, that she felt embarrassed. "It's just a scarf."

He opened his mouth to say something and then

closed it again and just shook his head. Emily followed his eyes, saw that he was watching the whole room, such a big, bright, smiling room, and she realized then what he was thanking her for. She had given him Christmas.

He looked at her again, and she nodded to show she understood. "You're welcome," she murmured, and they began to sing again, their voices joining together and becoming a part of the happiness of the room.

Valerie Hunter

Two Kinds of Christmas

Our new neighbor, Maria Sanchez, my little brother, Tommy, and I were building a wonderful sand castle at the beach. The hot sun was shining on the golden sand and blue water. Only, it wasn't summertime. Winter had begun, and Christmas was just a few days away.

Freckle-faced Tommy scooped up a handful of wet sand and shaped it into a ball. "Doesn't this look like a snowball, Bob?" he asked me. "It sure does," I agreed. "Why don't you put your sandball on top of our castle?"

"Then it will look like an ice cream sundae with a cherry on top," laughed Maria.

Suddenly, a big wave washed over the sand, and when it was gone, the castle had disappeared. Tommy

45

began to cry.

"Don't worry about the sand castle, Tommy," Maria said. "We can build a new one."

But Tommy cried even harder.

"Let's talk about Christmas, Tommy," I said. "You know how much you like cranberry cookies, decorating the tree, and hiding presents."

Tommy jumped to his feet. "There is no Christmas here!" he shouted. "There's no snow for sledding, no pine trees to trim, and our friends are far away!"

Now I knew why Tommy was so sad. We had just moved from our snowy Cape Cod home to a town near Mexico in southern California. Tommy missed the snow and his old friends. I missed those things, too, and I wondered what I could do to make him feel better.

"I have an idea," said Maria, her brown eyes sparkling. "My family is Mexican-American. Why don't you come to our Christmas party, called a *posada*, and find out how we like to celebrate the holiday?"

Tommy still looked glum when we arrived at Maria's home. Maria and her brother, José, who is the same age as Tommy, opened the door.

"Feliz Navidad!" greeted Maria. "Those are the

Spanish words for 'Merry Christmas.'"

"Hi Tommy! Hi Bob! Merry Christmas!" said José. "We hope you like our *posada*."

The Sanchez house glowed with lighted candles and bright paper flowers. We sat on the floor on striped rugs called *serapes* with the other excited children. Mrs. Sanchez brought bowls of popcorn for us to string.

"We make popcorn garlands for Christmas trees on Cape Cod, too," said Tommy, picking up a needle and thread. "But there are no Christmas trees here."

"Wait and see, Tommy," said Maria, giving me a secret smile.

We ate sweet cheese cookies, and because the day was warm, Mrs. Sanchez poured us each a glass of cold apple cider. "On Cape Cod we drink our cider hot," said Tommy doubtfully. He was still frowning, but he drank every drop of the cold cider and munched three of the unusual holiday treats.

When the garlands were finished, Mr. Sanchez carried a tall potted palm tree from the patio into the living room. "This is our Christmas tree," he said. "Let's put on the decorations."

The palm was shaped something like a pine tree,

but it had very long, stiff green leaves. After we hung a shiny blue ball on the tip of each sharp leaf, we draped the popcorn garlands around the palm.

Mr. Sanchez handed Tommy a glittering gold star, then lifted him high in the air. "Place the star at the top of the tree, Tommy," he said. With the star in place, everyone cheered.

Tommy almost grinned. "The palm is nearly as pretty as our Christmas trees back home," he decided.

Mr. Sanchez took a picture of all the children gathered around the palm, then Maria called out, "Papa, it's time for the *piñata!*"

The *piñata* was a clay jar covered with colored paper to look like a circus horse. It was filled with candy and small toys. Maria's parents dangled the *piñata* from a rope as each of us, wearing a blindfold, tried to break it with a stick. Tommy was the lucky one. When his turn came, he hit the jar and it burst open. Everyone laughed as they ran to pick up the candy and gifts. "This is fun," Tommy said, unwrapping a piece of candy and popping it into his mouth. "Too bad we didn't have *piñatas* on Cape Cod."

The next day, Mr. Sanchez drove us to the beach.

We splashed in the water and played tag on the sand while he took more pictures. Maria and José let us borrow their plastic foam surfboards. Tommy and I waded out into the ocean, lay down on our stomachs on the boards, and rode the waves back to shore.

"Surfing is a lot like sledding downhill in the snow," said Tommy, rubbing the salt water from his eyes. "Let's do it again!"

That night, we went Christmas caroling with Maria, José, and their friends. It seemed strange to wear shorts instead of snowsuits as we went from house to house singing "White Christmas" and "Jingle Bells" in English and Spanish. We had a good time, but I was still waiting for Tommy to smile.

The last stop was our house. Mom and Dad listened to us sing, then invited everyone inside for freshly baked cranberry cookies like we always ate on Cape Cod.

"You enjoyed the *posada* and the beach, didn't you, Tommy?" asked Mom.

"Oh, yes," he replied. "We made some new friends, but I still miss our old friends back home."

"I'll give you some of the pictures I took," said Mr. Sanchez. "Why not mail them to Cape Cod so they can see how we celebrate Christmas in the sun?"

"What about sending them an e-mail? Or calling on the telephone?" Dad suggested. "You can wish everyone *Feliz Navidad* and Merry Christmas."

"You could talk about sand castles and snowballs," laughed Maria.

"And pine trees and *piñatas*," I added.

"Don't forget surfing and sledding," said José.

At last, Tommy's face broke into a great big smile. "Wow! It's like having two kinds of Christmas!" he exclaimed. "There's more than one way to have fun on my favorite holiday. And I'm glad!"

Deborah Nigro

50

MISTLETOE MADNESS

Illustration by Elizabeth O. Dulemba

Lost!

Deer Lodge Valley, Montana – 1882

A cold, wet tongue woke Nate on a frosty December morning. He lay on his stomach across his wood-framed bed, and when he looked up through the darkness the first face he saw was Jack's. A pink tongue flopped out of the dog's mouth. Nate groaned and rolled over. The sun wasn't even up yet!

Jack whined.

Nate pulled his blanket over his head but Jack tugged it right back off. "All right, all right, I'm gettin' up." Nate laughed. Jack wagged his tail playfully.

"Do you want to play?" Nate waved the corner of

his blanket in front of the dog. "Come and get it." Jack bounced on his front paws. He jumped at the blanket and knocked them both to the floor.

"Nate, be quiet. I'm trying to sleep," Mabel Sue, Nate's ten-year-old sister, complained from across the room.

"I can't help it," Nate laughed. "Jack won't get off me."

"It would help if you didn't encourage him," Nate's mother said from the doorway. Her apron was covered in flour, and that could only mean one thing. Breakfast. Nate's stomach growled. He hoped it was flapjacks.

"Could you run out to the chicken coop and get me some eggs?" his mother asked.

"What are you making for breakfast? I'm starved."

His mother smiled. "Get the eggs and you'll find out."

Nate dressed quickly in the chilly morning air. He pulled on his patched coat and headed out the door with Jack. Shoving his hands under his armpits, Nate tucked his chin into his coat collar and crunched through the deep snow. The sun was shining now and it made the snowflakes glitter like silver. Nate opened his mouth and caught a few on his tongue. They melted instantly.

"C'mon, Jack." Nate raced him to the barn and swung the door open.

"Hello, son," Nate's father called as they entered the warm barn. He was sitting on a stool milking their cow, Bessie.

"Good morning, Pa. It sure is cold out, huh?" Nate slammed the door shut.

His father nodded. "It is cold. I think we might be in for another storm before the day is over."

Nate's heart sank. "Do you think Uncle Pete and Aunt Rose will still come out?" he asked.

Nate's aunt and uncle were supposed to come to the ranch that afternoon. They were going to stay the night so they could all spend Christmas Day together. Nate was especially excited for John to get there. His nine-year-old cousin was just Nate's age and Nate wanted to show him Jack's new tricks.

"I don't know," his father said.

Nate decided that he and Jack had better practice their tricks one more time, just to be sure they had them right. He whistled and Jack ran over to him.

"Jack, speak," Nate said.

Jack barked twice and wagged his tail.

"Jack, roll over."

The collie rolled over. He bounced back up and waited for Nate to give another command.

Nate bit his lip. Here was the test. "Jack, play dead." Jack lay down on the floor. He didn't move an inch.

"Good job," Nate praised him. Jack barked loudly and Nate's father frowned.

"Nate, take him outside if he's going to bark. I don't want Bessie to spill this pail of milk."

"All right," Nate said. "I'm going to get some eggs for Ma and go back to the house. Do you need me to do anything?"

"Just be sure the chicken coop door is shut when you are done."

"Okay." Nate buttoned his coat and went back outside with Jack. The snow was falling faster now. He hurried to get the eggs.

The chicken coop wasn't as warm as the barn, so Nate didn't waste time finding the eggs and putting them in his pocket. Just as he was closing the door, Jack began barking. The noise scared the chickens and they began to squawk. One of the hens flew out the door.

"Oh, no," Nate groaned. He latched the door and struggled through the snow after the flyaway bird. "Come back here."

Nate was upset, but Jack thought this was great fun. He chased the chicken across the yard and past the house. Before Nate knew what to do, they had disappeared into the swirling snow.

Nate raced after them. "Jack, get back here!" The wind and the snow were blowing so hard he could barely see in front of him and soon he was lost in a blur of white.

"Jack, where are you? Jack?" Nate was worried. What if Jack was lost? Nate called until his voice was hoarse. He was about to give up when he saw Jack running toward him through the snow. "Shame on you, Jack. What were you chasing that crazy chicken for?"

Nate grabbed Jack and turned back toward the ranch. He felt the eggs in his pocket to make sure they weren't broken. His mother would have enough to say about the lost chicken; he didn't want to come back empty-handed too.

"Come on, Jack, let's get back home. I'm cold."

MISTLETOE MADNESS

He lowered his head against the wind, his teeth chattering. Jack followed close by, rubbing his fur against Nate's leg. Nate was grateful for that touch. Jack was a good dog.

After they walked for fifteen minutes, Nate began to get worried. Shouldn't they have made it back to the house by now? Had they walked right past it in the blinding snow? Nate stood still and listened for a familiar sound. But all he could hear was the howling wind. How far had they walked?

"J-Jack, I t-think we're l-lost." Nate's lips seemed frozen together and he struggled to talk. The big dog whined and buried his nose under Nate's hand. The two friends stood there in silence. What if they couldn't find their way home?

Jack started pushing his nose against Nate's legs.

"W-What's the m-matter, boy?"

But Jack wouldn't quit. He pushed Nate until he'd finally nudged his master forward. Nate's legs felt stiff and strange, but he stumbled along. The snow drifts were past his knees now.

On they walked until they came to a group of tall pine trees. Jack pawed at the snow underneath the branches. Nate watched him curiously. Jack was digging a cave for them! Nate fell to his knees beside his dog and started to push the snow to the side. Once they cleared it away, they crawled beneath the branches and huddled together.

It was better under the tree. The snow was piled thick and high around them, blocking the stinging wind. Nate buried his face in Jack's fur and hugged him tight. It made his face warm. They sat under the tree for a long time. Nate was scared. What if they couldn't find their way back home?

Nate thought about that for a minute. It was Christmas Eve. Tomorrow would be Christmas Day. What if he missed it? He'd never missed Christmas with his family before. It was a sad thought. He and Mabel Sue and John always woke extra early that special morning. His mother and Aunt Rose would have breakfast prepared, and as soon as all the chores were done they'd gather around the fireplace while his father read about the birth of Christ.

Then they'd open presents. He wondered if Mabel Sue would like the book he got for her this year. Then he wondered what she'd gotten him. He'd certainly given her enough hints about the marbles they'd seen in the

MISTLETOE MADNESS

mercantile.

Nate's stomach growled and thoughts of Christmas faded. He was too hungry to think about presents. He wanted food. He pictured his mother in their nice, warm kitchen, making mountains of steaming flapjacks. His mouth watered and he could almost taste the yellow butter and sticky syrup.

He put his hands into his pockets for warmth and was surprised when he felt the cold, round eggs. "Jack, we have food!" Nate cried. He pulled the eggs from his pocket as Jack wagged his tail. If they could build a small fire, they could cook the eggs. Nate spotted some sticks and brushed the snow from them as he laid them in a pile. But then he realized they had no matches to start a fire with. His eyes watered and he rubbed them with a fist. He wasn't going to cry.

Instead, he patted Jack's head and put the eggs back into his pockets carefully. Jack laid his head on Nate's lap and looked at him with sad, brown eyes.

"We've got to think of something. I'll bet you're hungry, too." But Nate couldn't come up with any ideas. Finally he took one of the eggs from his pocket and looked at it long and hard. "We're going to have eat it

59

raw," he told Jack.

Jack looked at Nate.

"I know. I don't like the thought of it, either. But we are going to starve if we don't."

Nate rubbed the brown shell. This was going to be disgusting. He almost put the egg back in his pocket, but then his stomach growled and Nate knew what he had to do. He cracked the egg on his knee and tilted his head back. It plopped into his mouth in one giant, slimy clump. Nate made a face and swallowed.

Yuck! He shuddered and threw the eggshell onto the ground. Then he grabbed a handful of snow and ate it quickly. The snow melted in his mouth. It helped the last of the egg to go down his throat.

Nate pulled another egg out of his pocket and looked at his dog. Jack whined and buried his head in the snow. "Aw, Jack. You have to eat it. If I can eat an egg, you can too. You'll starve if you don't." He cracked the egg and let it plop in the snow. Jack licked it up.

"That wasn't so bad, now. Was it?"

Suddenly, Jack's ears stood up straight and he growled low in his throat. His bright yellow eyes looked past the low pine branches. Nate moved a branch and looked out, but he couldn't see anything except the falling snow. He couldn't hear anything either, but he knew that dogs could hear better than people.

"What is it, Jack? What do you see?" Nate whispered.

Jack sniffed the air. He growled again and this time his teeth were showing.

Nate backed up as close as he could to the tree. The bark was rough and cold. Then he heard the noise. It was the sound of footsteps crunching loudly in the snow. But they didn't sound like a person's footsteps, they were too loud. They sounded like an animal's footsteps. A large animal.

Then Nate heard the roar of a bear! Just past the trees a large brown bear stood on his back feet, sniffing the air. He was the tallest bear Nate had ever seen. His fur was matted and dirty. He looked thin—and hungry. Nate remembered his father telling him that sometimes bears woke during hibernation if they hadn't found enough food before winter. Nate just hoped he wouldn't be the bear's supper.

The bear looked around the trees, slowly moving toward Nate and Jack. "I think he can smell us," Nate whispered to his dog.

Jack growled again.

"Shh, Jack." Nate sat as still as he could and prayed that the bear wouldn't find them. He held his breath as the bear came closer. The bear looked around the clearing, but when he didn't see anything, he walked back out into the storm again.

When he was finally gone Nate let his breath out. "That was close," he told Jack. He rubbed the dog's head and snuggled close to his warm side. They sat under the tree for the rest of the day and watched the snow fall.

* * *

A cold, wet tongue woke Nate the next frosty morning. Nate pushed Jack's head away with a laugh. "Do you always have to wake me up that way?" he asked his dog. Nate stretched his muscles and looked out.

"Jack, it stopped snowing," Nate cried. He crawled out from beneath the pine branches. Jack followed him and shook the snow from his fur.

The sky was clear and blue this morning. The snow had stopped falling, but the drifts were high. The only sound Nate could hear was a woodpecker in the tree above him. Nate looked around. He'd hoped that once it stopped snowing he would be able to see the ranch. But he couldn't see anything that looked familiar.

"What are we going to do?" He asked Jack.

Jack was sniffing the air. He walked a few steps and sniffed again. He looked at Nate and barked loudly. Nate saw a movement from the corner of his eye. He turned around and gasped. Only a few yards away stood the same brown bear they had seen the night before. This time the bear saw him and he growled. Nate was too scared to move.

Jack raced toward the bear, barking wildly. The bear bellowed at Jack and swiped at him with his huge paw. But Jack was too fast. He barked and growled at the bear until the bear started backing away from Nate. Finally the bear grew tired of Jack's barking and ran into the thick trees.

Jack didn't chase him. He ran back to Nate and licked his face.

"Thanks, Jack," Nate said, hugging the dog tight.

Jack didn't stay still for long. Just like before, he began pushing at Nate's legs with his head, getting him to walk through the snow. Nate walked as fast as he could, but the snow was even deeper than before and he became tired quickly. Every few minutes Nate had to sit down and rest.

While he rested, Nate prayed. "God, thank you for protecting us from that bear. I was really scared. Jack and I are still lost though. We can't find the way home by ourselves. Please help us to trust You." When Nate was finished, he followed Jack again.

The morning quickly turned to afternoon and Nate's stomach growled. He almost wished for more eggs to eat. Almost. Instead, he ate handfuls of snow and daydreamed about every delicious meal his mother ever made. He could smell a beef roast covered in dark gravy. He could see loaves and loaves of fresh-baked bread. But most of all, he could almost taste his ma's flapjacks.

He was so busy dreaming that he almost didn't hear the voices. Voices! It sounded like his pa!

"Pa! Pa! I'm over here," Nate shouted. He stumbled through the snow.

"Nate? Nate!" his father shouted through his tears. He ran up to Nate and hugged him. "We were worried about you. Are you all right?"

Nate's uncle was with him. He reached over and messed up Nate's hair. "We've been looking for you all day."

Nate told his father and uncle about the chicken and how he and Jack had gotten lost. He told them about the bear and how Jack had chased it away too.

Nate's father pet the dog. "Jack's a good dog, Nate. You couldn't find a better friend."

When they got back to the ranch, Nate's mother promised to make him anything he wanted. The very first thing he asked for was flapjacks.

"Are you sure you don't want eggs?" she asked him.

Nate shook his head. "I don't know if I'll ever want to eat eggs again," he said.

They celebrated Christmas that night, and Nate was glad that Mabel Sue liked the present he'd gotten her. He didn't even care that she'd gotten the ten marbles for him that he'd wanted. He was just happy to be home with his family again.

Paula Miller

Texas Snow

I'm in Texas, where are you?
Do you have ice? 'Cause we sure do!
Do you have lots and lots of snow?
I know we sure don't!
We do get lots of mistletoe.
And kissing parents, ew oh no!
Here it rains and rains and rains
Even though it's Christmas day.
Every single night I pray
For it to snow on Christmas day!
So now, I search for snow
She will not come
She doesn't want to play!
But ice is here, and sleet is too
They've been here for days and days!

Lucia de León

MISTLETOE MADNESS

Illustration by Elsbet Vance

The Transformation of the Innkeeper

Two thousand years ago Bethlehem was not the busy, traffic-jammed, high-rise city it is today. It was a sleepy village of box-like mud dwellings lining dirt paths laid out by meandering goat herds. It was to this sleepy little town that the descendents of King David came to be counted in the census. With their arrival the village became a symphony of noise: camels moaning and grunting, donkeys braying, goats bleating, and boys calling to one another as they raced through the marketplace.

Noise was not the only problem. Bethlehem was

full and overflowing. Overcrowding was evident everywhere: too many people and too many animals. Everything was in a state of chaos because of the census.

The innkeeper had turned people away for days, and he was getting rude in his dealings with the late-comers. Usually irritable and curt, the innkeeper's nature was worse than usual. He had the disposition of a man with a serious case of indigestion, and he was fighting a headache worse than any he remembered.

On top of that, his daily routine was upset. The time it took to complete any task was multiplied. Even a simple task like going for water was no longer simple. He had to go for water more often, and each trip took longer than before because there was always a long line of people and animals waiting for a cooling drink. After three days he decided to do something about the long delays. He bellowed to the waiting crowd, "I will no longer wait in this line." He tried to cut in at the head of the line saying, "I am a busy man. I need my water NOW!" People all the way up and down the line complained. As the innkeeper pushed his way in front of the baker, the baker resisted. Two travelers joined the baker in the struggle. The innkeeper took a swing at someone. When the dust settled, the innkeeper had a place at the end of the line.

The small inn had filled quickly; still, the people kept coming. Perhaps another person could have dealt with futile requests for housing with more tact and patience. But it was the innkeeper's nature to be short-tempered. He was true to form, rudely slamming the door in the face of travelers who arrived after the inn was full. He rudely rejected a particular young couple when they came seeking shelter, by saying, "A room! You want a room? What do you think all these other folks want? Fresh fruit?" This feeble attempt at humor was about the only thing that pleased the ill-natured innkeeper.

His daughter, who had seen and heard everything, tried to get his attention; she had a solution. But her father ignored her, continuing to ridicule the young couple and their request. Just as the persistent housefly eventually gets your attention, the daughter finally penetrated her father's long, noisy scolding. "Father, the cave where the animals sleep is at least dry. It gives protection against the weather and the cold wind. Why can't these people stay there for the night?"

"What is that to me?" growled the innkeeper, "I

don't get paid for letting people sleep with the animals." And he slammed the door as he reentered the inn.

In spite of her father's objections the innkeeper's daughter led the young couple to the cave that would provide them protection for the night. The man was hesitant, not at the thought of sleeping among the hay and grain, nor at the thought of sleeping with the animals. He was cautious about accepting any lodging from the ill-natured innkeeper, but the woman, who was tired, pleaded with him. "The animals seem very accepting; if it is okay with them, why should we object? It isn't as though we had another choice."

So, it was there in a cave which served as a home for a goat and a few donkeys that the woman gave birth to a baby.

At the very time the baby was born, a brilliant light appeared in the sky. Villagers and travelers followed the light to understand where it was coming from and what it might mean. The star led them to the cave. When they saw the starlight shining down on the mother and baby, they whispered to each other, "Who are these people? They must be very special."

As the crowd grew, the whispering increased.

MISTLETOE MADNESS

Finally the noise reached a level the innkeeper could no longer ignore. Something was happening out back. He went to investigate, demanding as he went, "What is all the ruckus about?"

He had just stepped out the door when he was flooded in light. He saw the star which caused him to wonder. Then when he saw the people gathered around something in the cave, he had to know what was going on. Elbowing his way through the mass of people, he ruthlessly made his way to a place where he could see a woman holding a baby. He saw right away there was something special about the baby.

Instantly a glow swept through him, starting at the top of his head and passing down to his smallest toe. He felt warmed in a strange way. He felt as he never remembered feeling before. Just seeing this special baby filled the innkeeper's heart with love. His realization of the love surrounding the baby left him caring for others with the same kind of love. There was love in everything he did. He turned to the man behind him, apologizing for having pushed in front of him. He was embarrassed when he remembered his treatment of the mother and father of the baby. Realizing the couple had no food and had no way to get food, he returned to his kitchen and gathered a supper for them.

When the innkeeper returned to the cave, his neighbors had joined the crowd. They were amazed to see the transformation in the innkeeper's behavior. They had never seen him so open and warm, actually caring. The cold, gruff, unyielding innkeeper was transformed. The neighbors hardly recognized the changed innkeeper. They did not understand what caused him to change, but they were eager to become acquainted with the transformed innkeeper who felt the romance of unconditional love.

Ardeen Fredrick

MISTLETOE MADNESS

Winter Wonderland

Hannah sat on the dock behind her house, dipping her toes in the water. Although it was early December, the temperature was still a balmy 78 degrees. As she felt the warm water on her feet, Hannah imagined the lake had frozen over and she was going to go ice skating. Of course, she knew this was impossible. It never got that cold in Florida. She read a story about it actually snowing in Orlando once, but in all her ten years, she had never seen so much as an icicle. A dragonfly landed on her shoulder and Hannah pretended it was a tiny snowflake.

"Come inside and get ready, Hannah. We're going to see Santa at the mall," Mom called from the backyard.

Hannah rolled her eyes. She was too big for Santa

MISTLETOE MADNESS

Claus. All she wanted for Christmas was snow. Lots and lots of snow. I doubt Santa will bring any from the North Pole for me, she thought. She slowly got up and walked back to the house.

When she got inside, Hannah saw her little brother, Justin, pulling on his best shoes. He was wearing his suit for church and beside him was an extremely long piece of paper. With his shoe halfway on, Justin hopped over to his sister. "Hurry up, Hannah! Get ready! I finished my list and I want plenty of time to tell Santa what I want this year."

Hannah whistled at the sight of the paper on the floor. "That's some list, Justin. You must be asking for every single toy in the store."

Justin, who now had his shoe on, laughed. "It's not just for me. I added a few things for Mom and Dad, too, so Santa would think I was a really good boy and bring me even more stuff."

Hannah laughed. Justin was pretty smart for a six year old. Hannah put her sandals on and ran a brush through her wind-blown hair. She didn't want to talk to Santa, but she did think it would be fun to see what Santa thought of Justin's list.

MISTLETOE MADNESS

When they arrived at the mall, Hannah stared at all the Christmas decorations. There were large wreaths with red ribbons, garlands, twinkling lights, and huge Christmas trees. One of the trees had crystal snowflakes and icicle ornaments on it. *I wonder what that stuff really looks like*, Hannah thought.

Since they had arrived shortly after the mall opened, the line for Santa wasn't terribly long. Justin ran through the ropes and took his place in line. "Come on, Hannah! Come tell Santa what you want for Christmas," Justin called.

"I ask for the same thing every year, Justin. Santa already knows what I want," Hannah said.

"What is it, Hannah? I'll ask for you," Justin said and pulled out his list.

"Snow, Justin. Just once, I want to have snow on Christmas morning."

"That's a good one!" Justin exclaimed and added his sister's wish to his list.

Hannah stood with her mom beside Santa's chair as Justin took his turn. Santa chuckled as Justin described in great detail all the things on his list. When he got to the end, Justin glanced over at Hannah and said, "See my sister, Hannah, over there? She really, really wants some snow for Christmas. She doesn't think you can do it, but you can do anything, can't you, Santa?"

Santa looked over at Hannah and smiled. He looked at Mom, who shrugged her shoulders. "I'll try my very best, Justin," said Santa. Justin smiled and ran over to his sister. "See, Hannah! Santa's going to bring you snow."

Hannah smiled wistfully and hugged her brother. Hannah, Justin, and Mom stayed at the mall a bit longer. Mom wanted to pick up a present to send to Grandma and Justin wanted to look at the toy store to make sure he hadn't missed anything. Hannah wanted to look at travel brochures and daydream about places that would have a white Christmas.

The next few weeks passed quickly. On Christmas Eve, Mom and Hannah baked cookies and Dad helped Justin wrap a few last-minute gifts. At 8:30, Dad said he was really tired and he was going to bed. "You kids should get some sleep, too. We want to get up early in the morning to see what Santa brought." Dad smiled at Mom and kissed Hannah and Justin good night.

Justin put two cookies on a plate and poured a tall

glass of milk. He grabbed a cookie for himself and placed his list next to the plate. "What are you doing?" Hannah asked. Justin laughed. "I'm making sure Santa knows whose house he's in." Hannah nodded. "Good thinking, Justin!" Justin hugged Mom and Hannah and ran to his room.

"Now that the boys are in bed, what shall we do, Mom?" Hannah asked.

Mom yawned. "I think we should get to bed. Justin will probably wake us all up at dawn," said Mom.

"But Mom! It's only 8:30," cried Hannah.

"Trust me, Hannah. You'll be glad you went to bed early tonight," said Mom.

Hannah shook her head like everyone was crazy and went to her room. She looked outside. A few leaves were on the ground but the sky was clear and the grass was still green. *Another Christmas without snow*, she sighed.

Just as Mom predicted, Justin woke up as the sun was coming up. "Wake up! Wake up! It's Christmas!" Justin shouted. The family walked bleary-eyed into the living room. Justin was playing with the new truck that Santa had left for him and Mom was sitting on the couch drinking coffee.

"Merry Christmas," Mom said with a smile.

"Merry Christmas," said Hannah. Where's Dad?"she asked.

Justin put down his toy. "Yeah. Where is Dad?"

Just then, Dad walked in with a huge grin on his face.

"Merry Christmas, Dad. Where were you?" Hannah asked.

Dad looked at Mom. "You mean you haven't seen your present yet?" Dad asked.

Hannah shook her head.

"Look outside." Dad said and led Hannah to the window.

Hannah couldn't believe her eyes. There, in her very own yard, was snow. Lots and lots of snow. It was everywhere. She rubbed her eyes. "It can't be! It can't!" said Hannah.

"Oh, it's real all right. Come on outside and see for yourself," laughed Mom and Dad.

Hannah stared, amazed at the piles of white snow covering her yard. She reached down to feel it. It was cold! It was real snow there in her very own yard. Hannah scooped up a clump of the icy snow and tossed it into the air.

"I don't understand! How can this be happening?" Hannah asked, amazed. Justin threw a snowball that hit Hannah's belly.

"Santa brought it, silly! I told you he could do it!"

"Not exactly, Justin. He had a little help," said Mom.

"Remember Mr. Thompson?" Dad asked.

"Isn't he the one who runs the children's theater?" Hannah said.

Dad nodded. "Well, I ran into him the other day while I was doing some last-minute shopping. He asked how everyone was and I told him we were all fine but you were really sad because you wanted it to snow. He told me that he had rented a snow machine for the theater's outdoor production of "A Christmas Carol." The theater is closed for the next few nights and he said if I came over after the last performance, I could use it."

Hannah hugged her dad tightly. "So that's why you said you were tired last night. You had to pick up the machine."

"Well, I wanted you to have a white Christmas

when you woke up," smiled Dad.

"This is the best Christmas present ever!" exclaimed Hannah and she ran off to play in her very own winter wonderland.

Tricia Mathison

81

Grandmas and Snowmen

"Over the river and through the woods," Hannah sang as she brushed her steamy breath off the car window.

Shut up, Hannah, I wanted to say. But if I did, Dad would have something to say to me.

"The horse knows the way," she continued.

"Are you calling me a horse?" Dad asked. Hannah giggled. Ever since we left home Hannah had been singing her cheery little Christmas songs. I wasn't in the mood for Christmas—not this year. Not when we were spending it at Grandma and Grandpa Watkins' house.

"Look, Mommy!" Hannah shrieked. "Mitford snowmen."

"Must be a contest," Mom suggested. "There's

one in every yard and each snowman is different."

"This isn't Mitford," I growled, giving Hannah a poke in the ribs. I stopped pouting long enough to glance at the snowmen.

Mom turned around as far as she could without unbuckling her seatbelt. "Emily, what's wrong with you? You've been a real grump since we left home."

"I'll tell you what's wrong," I shouted. "We're going to the wrong Grandma's. All Grandma Watkins gives us for Christmas is her homemade sweaters and mittens and stuff. And there's totally nothing to do at her house."

"That's enough," Dad said. I knew he meant it.

I slumped back down in my seat. There was nothing more to say.

Soon we reached the farm and Grandma met us at the back door. My grump began to melt away when she gave me a big soft hug. Also, I'd forgotten how good her house smelled, especially at Christmas time.

She'd been cooking and baking. I wondered if she'd made my favorite cookies again this year. They weren't exactly Christmas cookies, but some kind of brownie with a secret ingredient that made them special.

MISTLETOE MADNESS

While Dad brought our things in from the car, Hannah and I ran to the living room to check out the Christmas tree. Grandpa threw another log into the fireplace. He came over to give us each a hug. Another hunk of my grump hopped right off my shoulder and into the fire.

"Grandma Kelly lives in 'partment so she has a little tree," Hannah told Grandpa.

"Does she, now? We have a big house and I cut this big tree yesterday—just for you, Punkin."

Hannah giggled. "Grandpa! I'm not Punkin, I'm Hannah."

"So you are." Grandpa gave her another hug. "What do you think, Emily? Like the tree?"

I nodded, suddenly feeling ashamed about the way I'd acted in the car. If only it weren't for the presents. Grandma Kelly lives in the city and gives us lots of good stuff.

After lunch Mom went upstairs to unpack. Hannah tagged along after her. Dad and Grandpa settled down in front of the fireplace. Soon they began to snore. I hung around the kitchen with Grandma, glancing over all her Christmas goodies.

MISTLETOE MADNESS

Grandma said, "I haven't made your cookies yet, Emily. I thought you might like to help me and learn to do it yourself."

Grandma put everything we'd need on the table and told me what to do. While we worked, she said, "This year we have plenty of snow. Tomorrow afternoon Grandpa will get out the sleigh and we'll all take a ride in the fields. Would you like that?"

I knew I would. I thought about Hannah's Christmas songs and the snowmen in front of the houses. Each snowman was different, just like Mom said. Grandmas are different too. Grandma Kelly is a shopping Grandma. But Grandma Watkins is a cooking and knitting Grandma. At last I figured it out. Grandma Watkins' secret ingredient is love. She put love into the cookies she baked. She put love into the sweaters she knit for me.

My grump completely, totally disappeared.

Marion Tickner

MISTLETOE MADNESS

Emily's Favorite Cookies

What you'll need:
1 package Brownie Mix
Eggs, water, oil—as listed on the package
½ cup chocolate chips
½ cup peanut butter chips
½ cup shredded coconut
½ cup broken walnuts or pecans
What to do:
Preheat oven and prepare Brownie Mix according to directions on the package.
In a separate bowl, combine chocolate chips, peanut butter chips, coconut, and nuts.
Add one-half of the chips-coconut-nuts mixture to the Brownie batter.
Pour into greased baking pan and spoon the remainder of the chips-coconut-nuts mixture over the top of the batter. Bake per directions on the package. Cool. Cut into squares. Enjoy!

Marion Tickner

MISTLETOE MADNESS

Illustrations by Terri L. Sanders

The Stalking Snowman

"Wait up! I yelled at my older sister as she headed for school. "Don't leave!"

Lorraine paused and glanced back, but she didn't slow down. She hurried on, pretending she hadn't heard me.

I stood at the corner, huddled in my heavy blue coat while I waited for cars to stop whizzing by, feeling as wanted as an ice cube in Antarctica. Even worse, it was beginning to snow.

"Hey, Judi," my next-door neighbor, Peter, said as he came to stand beside me. "The ice-queen ditch you again?"

A lump stuck in my throat. I nodded.

"You don't need your stuck-up sister." A huge snowflake landed on his nose, and he brushed it away. "Everything about her is fake. She wears too much makeup. And she never goes anywhere without her brush and blowdryer. Just because she hangs with a popular crowd, she thinks it's okay to be a jerk."

"Yeah," I said quietly, wishing I could hang with the cool crowd. But they always froze me out. "Go away Tag-Along. Bug someone else," they'd taunt.

The traffic thinned, so we crossed the street. Peter said, "After school, let's have a snowball fight or make a snowman." He gave a sudden gasp. "Hey, look! Someone's already made one."

I followed his gaze to a bulging white snowman standing alone in the park. The snowman had a sharp carrot nose, a crooked stick mouth, and a blood-red hat perched on his head. His eyes were hidden by a pair of dark glasses.

I'll bet he's lonely, I thought. Then I smiled at my imagination. I even imagined that the snowman waved at me.

Gray skies and increasing snowfall trapped everyone inside during lunch. When I glanced out the cafeteria window, I saw a snowman that looked *exactly* like the one I'd seen in the park. I turned to point him out to a friend, but when I looked again, he was gone.

Okay, now this was weird.

When school ended, I overheard Lorraine planning to go ice skating with her friends. This was my chance! I wouldn't let them ditch me again, so I raced home to get my ice skates.

Afterwards, I glanced at Peter's house and saw a snowman in the front yard. When had Peter had time to build a snowman? And why did this snowman have a blood-red hat and crooked stick smile?

Feeling a chill in my spine, I headed to the outdoor rink. Once there, I saw Lorraine laughing with her popular friends. I called out her name twice, but she ignored me. Instead, she playfully tossed a snowball at a tall blond boy named Arty. He dodged it, and it sailed past, knocking a dark-red hat off a snowman.

The *same* snowman. Only now he was here at the skating rink—like he was stalking *me*.

"Mr. Snow lost his hat," I heard the blond boy call to my sister. "Cool shade of red. Too nice for a dumb snowman. I'm gonna keep it." He reached for the hat. But before he could grab it, the snowman's frosty arm shot out. Suddenly, Arty froze like a human popsicle.

Lorraine had been digging into her backpack and hadn't noticed the snowman. When she glanced over at Arty, she complained, "Stop kidding around and help me find my brush."

The snowman looked at my sister with a twisted stick scowl. He was alive and dangerous! But my clueless sister *still* hadn't noticed. I had to warn her.

I dropped my skates in the snow and ran forward. "Lorraine! Watch out!" But like always, she ignored me.

The burly white snowman reached out. His frosty fingers touched my sister. She froze, her pretty mauve-painted lips chilled in surprise. Icicles dripped from her perfect hair and her creamy skin turned wintry white. Her backpack fell, her brush rolling into the snow.

Other kids turned to look, gaped in horror, then screamed and fled. Terror filled me and I wanted to run, too. But I couldn't leave Lorraine.

"Judi!" I heard someone call, and saw Peter rushing forward.

"The snowman!" I screamed. "He froze my sister by touching her!"

"Stay away from him or he'll freeze you, too."

"But what about my sister?"

"We'll help her later. Now we have to get rid of the snowman. Maybe we can scare him away," Peter exclaimed, scooping up a handful of snow. "Let's nail him with snowballs."

I bent down and balled up snow. "Unfreeze my sister, you goon!" I shouted as Peter and I threw snowballs. But the snowballs stuck to the snowman and he grew larger. His stick scowl deepened. His gaze settled on me, and I could tell he was furious. He didn't speak, but I heard his thoughts in my head. "Being lonely made me angry. Anger made me alive. You could have been my friend, but you sided with them. Now you'll suffer."

Giving my frozen sister a helpless look, I grabbed Peter's hand. We ran. The snowman ran. I could hear his enormous snow steps stomp after us.

"He's . . . He's so fast! We'll never get away!" Peter stumbled over a snow pile. I yanked him up, and we kept running. We dashed around the ice rink, going in a big circle, panting with terror. The snowman almost grabbed my coat, but I dodged just in time. Then he grabbed for Peter. Suddenly, Peter's icy hand slipped from mine. I didn't stop, but I glanced over my shoulder and saw Peter lying in the snow . . . frozen.

And the snowman was right behind me!

I couldn't outrun him. He was too quick. So I made a desperate turn toward the ice rink. I plunged onto the slippery ice, falling to my knees, sliding wildly forward. The snowman stayed on the edge of the rink, raising his frosty arms in rage, but not stepping on the ice.

I ached all over. My fingers were numb. If I stayed here, I'd freeze, even without the snowman's icy touch. I kept sliding forward, toward my sister who stood still on the snow. I glanced around, desperate for escape.

An idea popped into my head. I hurried off the ice.

With the snowman circling the rink toward me, I dove for my sister's backpack. I found what I needed.

The snowman advanced toward me. His stick mouth twisted with fury. Icy anger sizzled through his dark glasses. He lifted his arm, one stubby snow finger reaching out to touch me.

I moved quickly and aimed something white and dangerous at him. My sister's battery-powered blowdryer. I pushed a button. A hot furnace of air spewed at the snowman. He shrieked. He backed away. But I moved forward, watching water drip from his arms, his legs, his face, his body, until there was nothing left but a stick, a carrot, glasses, and a blood-red hat.

Around me, kids began to thaw. Peter rushed over and high-fived me. "Congratulations! You did it!" he said. "Let's go celebrate with hot chocolate at my house."

"No," Lorraine objected, coming over with a wide smile. "She's going to hang with me and my friends. Aren't you, Judi?"

I grinned at my sister and shook my head.

Then I stepped over a pile of slush that once was a snowman and set off to get some warm, delicious hot chocolate with a good friend.

Linda Joy Singleton

Unexpected Guests

Doris pulled the lace curtain aside and peered out into the early morning gloom. Distant church bells were ringing in Christmas Day. Passersby, bundled in great coats, scurried along past the triple-decker houses, bending their heads against sudden gusts. Snow fell in giant flakes, which the wind, whistling and howling since dawn, beat against the windowpanes. She tugged her cardigan sweater closer about her and inhaled the aroma of turkey wafting from the oven—grateful she could stay put.

It had been a lonely year. Her husband had died last January. Oh sure, Doris enjoyed her knitting circle and church group, but this old house they had rented for twenty years just wasn't the same anymore. Today, however, would be different. Her son and his family were traveling down from their home up north.

Thumping noises from upstairs reminded her of her biggest problem. Ever since that woman and her three sons had moved in, Doris had felt nervous. The previous tenant had been quiet and away often.

Doris smoothed out the special linen cloth on the table for the third time and placed polished silverware at each setting of Christmas china. Everything looked perfect. Well . . . hopefully. Her daughter-in-law and grandchildren had pretty fancy tastes. They would think her artificial tree too small. Just last week, her grandson had told her about the massive tree they chopped down in the woods.

Doris bit her lip: if only they lived closer or visited more often. They certainly had busy schedules.

Her thoughts were interrupted by the telephone.

"Hi, Ma." It was her son, Wayne.

"Are you calling from around the corner on your cell phone?" Doris asked.

"No, Ma," Wayne said. "There's a major blizzard here."

"I see," said Doris, sinking into a chair at the decorated table.

"I've been out snow-blowing and just heard the main road is closed." Wayne paused. "Maybe next weekend, instead?" Doris heard her daughter-in-law in the background, prompting him.

"Or rather, sometime after New Year's," Wayne said.

"Whenever you can make it," Doris said, trying to sound hearty as she glanced at the snowman centerpiece. "I wouldn't want you to risk driving in bad weather."

"I'm real sorry, Ma. The kids will call later to tell you about their gifts."

"Merry Christmas to all of you," said Doris, struggling to get the last words out.

The house went dead silent, as quiet as it was at midnight when Doris would sometimes pace back and forth, checking door locks. Her eyes filled with tears when she heard the muffled notes of carolers going by. "Doris," she said to herself, "stop this at once before you start weeping all over your good tablecloth."

Thumping began upstairs again—bass vibrations from rock music.

MISTLETOE MADNESS

"I wonder if they're going anywhere," she thought and then remembered they didn't have a car. Much moving around was heard and, now, footsteps coming down the stairs.

Doris went to her front window and watched a woman step away from the doorway, pulling a worn coat around her. The woman looked up and down the street while snowflakes landed in her dark, wavy hair.

She turned and stepped back inside, her face younger and sadder than Doris had imagined. Doris waited to hear the footsteps going back up the stairs. Silence. Then a light rap.

Had she locked herself out or was the knocking on Doris' own door? Doris held her breath. Another knock. She moved to the door and opened it, the chain still in place across a two-inch gap.

"I'm sorry to bother you," the woman said. "I'm Maria . . . from upstairs. Could I please use your telephone?"

Doris hesitated.

"We have run out of heat," Maria said.

Doris unchained the door and only then noticed the curly-haired little boy peeking around his mother. She directed Maria to the phone, and looked at the boy whose large, bright eyes were taking in the whole room. Doris glanced around, too, then went over to plug in the tree.

"Come, José," the woman said moments later.

"Did you get help?" asked Doris.

"Nobody was there," said Maria, looking down. "Thank you and Merry Christmas."

She pulled José toward the door.

"Perhaps you could stay a while," Doris said, "until you get warm."

"We'll be okay," said Maria, ignoring José's tugging her in the other direction.

"It's no problem," said Doris. "My family is unable to come—because of the snow."

Maria hesitated. "My two other sons are upstairs."

Before Doris could get the proper words out, José exclaimed, "Maybe they can come here, too."

Doris swallowed hard, then nodded.

The first boy was about fourteen. He rubbed his frozen hands together while looking around, in much the same way José had. The oldest boy arrived in a T-shirt and shoved his way through the door, his bulky guitar slung over one shoulder.

MISTLETOE MADNESS

Doris felt her body stiffen. His eyes would not meet hers as he went to stand beside his mother.

"This is Carlos," said Maria, "he's a musician."

Doris resisted rolling her eyes. *If you want to call it that*, she thought, remembering the loud noise she often heard through the ceiling.

Conversation would have been difficult had José not turned out to be a little chatterbox. The youngest boy inspected each of Doris' decorations, especially the lighted church with tiny animals inside. Every few minutes José would jump up to peer into the church again.

When José's stomach growled, Doris remembered the food. They shoved chairs out of the way as she opened the oven door wide, pulling out baked potatoes, then the turkey. She lugged it to the table, glancing back to find all three boys watching. Then Maria announced it was time to go.

"Please help me eat all this," said Doris, reaching out to touch Maria's shoulder.

The younger woman looked at her sons and then nodded. Doris pulled more things out of the refrigerator. Maria ran upstairs for Portuguese sweet bread she had found at the food store.

MISTLETOE MADNESS

Doris felt an unexpected joy, watching them eat her food. Later, she passed out a few extra gifts she had gotten for her family.

Carlos still hadn't said much and when he reached for his guitar, Doris felt her anxiety return. She closed her eyes and waited.

The sweet notes of "Silent Night" suddenly filled the room.

Doris opened her eyes and looked from one guest to the next, her eyes finally coming to rest on Carlos, strumming away.

He took a quick peek at her, a mischievous grin appearing on his lips. Then he broke into the joyful sounds of *"Feliz Navidad."*

Marcia Strykowski

Christmas Conundrums:
Christmas Riddles

Perfumed pines
Sparkling with electric glitter.

Sparkling crystals
Sprinkled over ground and branches.

Sprinkled gold icing
Decorating sweet butter stars.

Decorating boxes
Hidden surprises filled with care.

Christmas trees light long, cold nights.
Snow falls quietly to the ground.
Golden cookies frosted with ice.
Presents wrapped for family with love.

Christine Gerber Rutt

MISTLETOE MADNESS

Illustration by Elizabeth O. Dulemba

The Remarkable Christmas Package

This story was inspired by a notice in a Vermont newspaper in January 1907, describing a little girl's recent Christmas present.

"Dorie!" Mr. Cady called up the stairs. "I'm hitching up Prancer!"

Mrs. Cady stirred the fire in the kitchen stove. "I don't think you should have told her, Samuel," she said. While the house was quiet and no one was poking around in her cupboards, she intended to finish her baking. She tied her apron on firmly, adding, "Now it won't be a surprise."

"I only said there was a package for her," her husband replied, "coming on the train from Portland. That's all I said." He tucked in his scarf and looked out the window. There wasn't a flake on the ground, but the air was crisp—maybe from the North Pole, he said to himself, considering the day of the year.

"Dorie!" Mr. Cady called again.

As she did every morning, Mrs. Cady took a stub of pencil and drew a line through the previous day on the calendar. With a sure hand, she marked off December 23, 1906. That left December 24th staring her, undeniably, in the face. She surveyed the bowls of maple sugar, candied fruit, and shelled black walnuts on the table. December 24th—and so much baking yet to do.

With his hand on the doorknob, Mr. Cady began, "Tell her—" But there was Dorie, scampering down the stairs, bundled up in the green winter coat that was too small for her now.

"I'm ready, Pa," Dorie announced. Her eyes bubbled with excitement.

"Did you put on those long johns that I set out for you?" her mother asked. "It's cold out there, and the station is a fair jaunt."

"I'm as snug as a bear cub in its den, Ma," Dorie said. She wore the wool mittens her mother had just made for her from layers of cloth cut up from an old pair of her father's trousers. Dorie had placed her hands flat on the kitchen table while her mother had traced around them with a piece of chalk. Then Ma had recited the verse she always repeated at such times: "Use it up, wear it out. Make it do, or do without."

This was the year that Dorie had learned to knit, too. She wore her first accomplishment: a long blue scarf, just the color of her eyes. It had turned out longer than she had planned. But this was a perfect day for her scarf, for she could wrap it over her head and twice around her neck and still have enough to tuck in. Her mother slipped the ends between Dorie's coat buttons.

"Are you making something special, Ma?" Dorie asked.

Mrs. Cady's eyes betrayed a twinkle. "I am, indeed," she said. "I just have a feeling it's going to be a remarkable Christmas this year."

"That train's coming," Mr. Cady reminded, "with us or without us."

Mrs. Cady cautioned, as Dorie dashed to her father's side, "You two come straight back. I don't like that sky."

"You never do, Lydia," Mr. Cady said dryly, as he and Dorie slipped outside.

Soon the big chestnut horse, Prancer, was pulling the wagon neatly over the winding road toward the village.

"I'll be glad of a little snow," Mr. Cady said. "It'll keep the dust down on the road. It's as bad as summertime." Winter or not, the wagon stirred billows of dust into the air that tumbled into the pastures on both sides of the road.

"Not too much snow," Dorie called over the clatter of the wagon. "We might not reach the depot."

"Oh, we'll be there in a snap," her father replied.

"Is it a big package, Pa?" Dorie asked.

Mr. Cady tilted his head to one side. "Since I haven't laid eyes on it, I can't say *exactly* how big or how small it might be. It's coming from Portland, Maine. That I can tell you."

Dorie knew that near Portland, Maine, was where her grandparents—Ma's folks—lived. She wondered what

might be likely to come from so far away. As they crossed
the bridge, she looked down and saw the web of ice spun
over the stream and the ghost of the water flickering under
it. They passed a neighbor's sugarhouse at the bend in the
road. Then just ahead they saw a woman standing in the
road, waving in their direction. She was wrapped in a
heavy brown shawl and carried a bundle shaped like a
baby in a blanket.

"Pa," Dorie said, "it's Mrs. Pease."

As they approached, they saw Mrs. Pease was not
carrying a baby but a bundle, wrapped neatly in paper and
twine.

"Betsy!" Mr. Cady called, pulling Prancer to a
stop. "Anything the matter? It's not Isaac, is it?'

"'Morning, Samuel, Dorie," Mrs. Pease greeted
them. "No, my husband's as good as can be expected. I
just remembered Lydia's saying you were meeting the
White River train this morning—hoped I didn't miss
you."

"That's right," Mr. Cady said. "We have a special
package coming on the 9:20."

Mrs. Pease smiled. "I heard something about a
package."

MISTLETOE MADNESS

Dorie told her, "It's coming from Portland, Maine—from Grandma and Grandpa."

"Oh, that'll be a Christmas package," Mrs. Pease replied. "Must be an unusual one to be coming on the train all that way." Her smile then faded. "I got a parcel here, too." She held out the bundle. "My niece has decided to get married tomorrow evening—Christmas night—before her young man goes off in the army. She hasn't got a wedding dress, and when I heard, well, my Alice's dress was upstairs packed away. They're just the same size, so we want my niece to have it, a real wedding dress." She added sadly, "You know I can't leave Isaac the way he is since he had his spell or I'd take it myself. Could you ask them to put it on the train for Woodstock? My sister's husband will come out from the farm to get it."

"My," Mr. Cady said, "a wedding dress."

"I could carry it," Dorie offered. "That *is* an important package."

"We'll see it gets safely to the depot," Mr. Cady promised, as Dorie took the parcel in her arms. "We better step on it, too," he said. He gave the reins a brisk shake and they set off, waving goodbye.

MISTLETOE MADNESS

Prancer's lively pace soon brought them to the village, past the tall white church on the green, the houses on Main Street, Parkers' store, the post office, and the inn. When they turned the corner, the depot lay straight ahead and the train had yet to arrive.

"Wait here, Dorie," Mr. Cady said, jumping out of the wagon and tying up the horse. "Henry!" he called to the stationmaster who was tacking a notice on the schedule board.

"Samuel," the stationmaster replied, "looking for Santy Claus?"

"Just about," Mr. Cady replied. "We've got a package on the White River train."

The stationmaster tapped his last tack with a small hammer he then slipped in his pocket. "Oh, that'll be the Montreal Flyer." His voice dropped. "Sorry, Samuel. The Flyer had a boiler problem. They switched everybody over to the Rutland train to catch the Montreal Express coming up from Bennington."

"Rutland," Mr. Cady repeated. "The freight, too? It's a special package," he added, casting a glance toward Dorie in the wagon.

"Oh, a Christmas package," the stationmaster

guessed. "I see." He gestured toward the notice he had just posted. "They wired they were bringing everything by Rutland. Not likely the freight will get to us today—too late for the 1:06 this afternoon. But tomorrow," he began but then stopped himself. "Oh, no, not on Christmas. Holiday schedule." He gave the matter some thought. "I believe though," he started in again, taking out a well-thumbed little yellow book and rustling the pages, "yes, that train'll stop in Woodstock."

"Woodstock, you say?" Mr. Cady exclaimed.

"But you'll have to step on it, Samuel."

Mr. Cady rushed to the wagon, whisking the reins free.

"Pa, Mrs. Pease's parcel!" Dorie reminded.

Her father turned Prancer toward Main Street, and the wagon wheels began to spin. "We're going to deliver it ourselves!" he replied, as they veered around the corner.

The road to Woodstock was a long, lonely ride. The Cadys had just passed the halfway mark when the first snowflakes began to fall, thick and fast. Mr. Cady had to slow Prancer to a careful pace. Soon the road ahead turned white with snow. "Whoa," Mr. Cady called to the horse, slowing Prancer's trot even more. "Looks like your mother was right about that sky," he told Dorie.

"She usually is," Dorie replied. "I suppose my present will be just as nice after Christmas, if we have to turn back." She knew she had to say this, even though her heart was filled with curious excitement about her mysterious package. Pa would know what was best, and she didn't want him to feel bad about whatever he thought they should do.

"Well, we're not that far now," he said. "Might as well go on just a bit. I only hope we're not going to miss that train. Prancer will get us there safely, and that's what counts."

But around the next corner they found another group of travelers who had not been so fortunate. Three men stood clustered at the side of the road, staring at something.

"Somebody in the ditch, Pa?" Dorie asked.

"Looks like it," Mr. Cady said, as a big burly man walked to the center of the road and held up his hand to stop them. They could see the wagon was a large one, and its rear axle was snapped right in two. The wagon had been hauling something in a large, dark crate.

"Thank goodness you come along," the big, burly

man said. "We're in a pickle."

"Anybody hurt?" Mr. Cady asked.

"With the possible exception of Reverend Waterman's pump organ, I'd say no," the man replied.

A short, plump man, with snow accumulating on his bare head, came forward. He wiped the snow off the round lenses of his eyeglasses. He introduced himself and shook hands with Mr. Cady. "Reverend Waterman," he said. "We hoped to use this organ for Christmas Eve service," he explained. "Widow Nipps, up the road, was kind enough to donate it to the church—in South Pomfret." He motioned down the road.

"Was it hurt, the organ?" Dorie asked. She felt sorry for the pump organ, tilting unhappily in the ditch.

Rev. Waterman wiped his glasses again, but the snowflakes kept sliding down them like tears. "Looks okay," he answered. "I see you folks got an empty wagon," he remarked.

"We're hoping," Mr. Cady explained, "to catch the train from White River."

The big, burly man took out his pocket watch, shielding the face from the falling snow with his hand. "You'll have missed it in two minutes, and you still got some miles to go yet, I'm sorry to say."

Dorie was determined to hide her disappointment. "We still have an important package to deliver," she said, holding out the bundle with the wedding dress inside. She felt some comfort knowing *someone* would get a special package that day.

"But," her father admitted, "I guess we got time to help you folks out, since we haven't that far to go." He jumped out of the wagon and helped the men lift the pump organ into the back of the wagon. Rev. Waterman insisted on sitting himself down beside it, as if to guard the pump organ from any further disaster. His two companions remained to unhitch their horse and walk him home before dealing with the broken axle. When they reached the Congregational Church in South Pomfret, Rev. Waterman brought Dorie and her bundle inside to sit by the stove that was just starting to warm the church. By the time the organ was unloaded and brought up the steps to the church, Dorie was toasty warm again.

The wheels of the wagon now sank into the snow, leaving dark tracks, as they made their way toward Woodstock. "I hope this stops soon," Mr. Cady said. The snowflakes had turned to heavy clusters. "What will your

MISTLETOE MADNESS

mother be thinking back home?"

They found the stationmaster shoveling off the train platform at the Woodstock depot. "Missed it," he confirmed, listening to Mr. Cady's story. "Christmas package, you say? Too bad." He smiled at Dorie.

"We have another Christmas package," Dorie volunteered, bringing out the bundle she had wrapped in the tail ends of her long scarf.

"Ah," exclaimed the stationmaster, studying the handwriting on the bundle. He shouted down the platform, "Mr. Todd! I believe this'll be for you!" A farmer with snow on his hat strode toward them. He shook hands with Mr. Cady and took the parcel from Dorie's arms.

"Won't my wife and daughter be delighted," Mr. Todd said. "Thank you, young lady—thanks to both of you."

"Good thing you were coming this way," the stationmaster said. "Who knows when, or if, that afternoon train will be coming, if this keeps up 'til then. I'm just sorry you missed your Christmas parcel, that's all."

"I'm so grateful to you folks," Mr. Todd repeated.

115

"It's not just the dress. We're going to miss Betsy and Isaac at the wedding. This'll be like having 'em there, in a way." He looked out at the snow. "You're not headed back to Bethel in this . . . with that wagon? Come out to the farm. Jessie and I would love to have you."

"I guess we can make it," Mr. Cady replied, "if we take it good and slow. Thanks just the same. Home's the place for Christmas Eve."

A boy called from the ticket window, "Mr. Willard. This just come in." He waved a paper toward the stationmaster.

The stationmaster pored over the telegram. "Uh oh," he said. "Load of logs from the sawmill up in Bridgewater tipped over on the tracks. Hills must be icy. We're to hold all trains until further notice 'til they get it cleared up."

"Would that be holding up the Rutland train?" Mr. Cady asked, suddenly interested.

The stationmaster popped open the lid of his watch. "Oh, yes. That won't even get there for a quarter of an hour. You'd catch that train in Bridgewater. They'll be lucky to get moving again before dark—that is, if you can get through."

MISTLETOE MADNESS

Mr. Todd suddenly jumped in with a suggestion. "Say, tell you what. I've brought the sleigh. Let me take your wagon out to the farm. It's just four miles, and I can do that easy. You take my sleigh—you take it—and we'll exchange whenever we get the chance. I'd like to do whatever I can for your Christmas, too."

"Oh, can we, Pa?" Dorie pleaded. "With a sleigh, we can go like lightning."

"A sleigh," Mr. Cady murmured. As carefully as he could, without saying too much, he explained, "See, I brought this wagon on purpose. This Christmas package on the train, coming from Maine . . ."

Mr. Todd interrupted, "Is that big enough for you?" He pointed to a sleigh down by the end of the platform. There, decorated with white, lacy snow, sat an enormous red, three-seater sleigh. "I brought this big old thing out of the barn in case any wedding guests turned up on the train. Doesn't look like I'll need it anyway."

Mr. Cady studied the sleigh and nodded. "All right, but let's trade horses," he said cheerfully. "I know Prancer's ways—and he could find his way through any snow."

In moments the two men had traded horses and

117

vehicles and Dorie found herself lifted into the front seat of the big sleigh. "I feel like Santa Claus's helper," she said, laughing.

"Bridgewater!" the stationmaster suddenly exclaimed. "Wait a moment, I near forgot!" He emerged again from the depot, carrying a white square box neatly tied up with string. "Since you're headed in that direction, there's a lady in Bridgewater Corners having her birthday tomorrow. She'll be a hundred years old!"

"A hundred!" Dorie exclaimed. "That's a lot of birthdays."

"This is her cake," the stationmaster said. "A young woman brought this in to send up this afternoon, but I'm not that hopeful about it getting there."

"We'll take it and put it on the train," Mr. Cady suggested. "There might even be someone at the depot headed that way faster than that." He accepted the white square parcel. "Let's give it to Dorie. She's good at delivering packages."

In short order, Prancer was at the head of the old sleigh as Mr. Cady and Dorie sailed down Woodstock's Main Street like a child on ice skates. They glided over the bridge and out into the country again, following the river that ran black and winding through the white snow.

About a mile from town they caught up with a man walking by the side of the road and knew him at once to be a doctor from the kind of satchel he was carrying. Mr. Cady pulled Prancer to a stop.

"I was just down to the post office," the doctor explained. He was a young man with cheeks turned rosy by the cold. "A call came in for me there—a woman's having a baby up the way a few miles. Likely it's twins. They run in the family."

"We're headed to Bridgewater," Dorie explained, "and we've got lots of room."

"Why it's right by there," the doctor replied. "I wouldn't turn down a ride. Save me going back and hitching up my team. I can always get a ride back." He climbed up in the sleigh. "Thanks!"

They hadn't gone two miles farther before Dorie exclaimed, "What's that on the riverbank, Pa?"

The doctor leaned forward and tapped Mr. Cady's shoulder. "Somebody's got an automobile and it's slid off the road. We better stop and see if I'm needed." As they neared they could see the large black automobile lying on its side like a sick cow.

MISTLETOE MADNESS

Mr. Cady shook his head at the sight. "Nothing more foolish than trying to get around in one of those things this time of year. Sensible people put a thing like that up in the barn on blocks 'til spring. Lucky they didn't end up in the river."

The doctor agreed, "They'll never make one that'll match a good horse."

When the sleigh pulled up to the scene, three people walked around from behind the toppled vehicle. They were Boston people on the way to Rutland for Christmas. They were grumbling to themselves, but otherwise unharmed. The driver was a stout man in a fine tweed coat, who stood with his fists on his hipbones, glaring at the automobile as if it were a naughty child. Two ladies stood by: his wife, a thin lady in a tall hat with arching feathers, and his wife's sister, a small woman with a fox stole wrapped around her neck. Dorie stared at the fox whose little jaws snapped its own tail.

Mr. Cady and the doctor urged them into the sleigh. "If the train's going to be stuck in Bridgewater overnight," Mr. Cady said, "I'm sure someone will put you up. You'll freeze out here."

"Thank heavens you have a big sleigh," said the

lady in the tall hat, as the doctor helped her up. "We have a parcel to bring with us, too."

Dorie asked, "It isn't a special Christmas parcel, is it?"

"Why, yes, my dear," she replied. "It's my grandson's first Christmas. They live in Rutland."

Mr. Cady helped the man extract a handsome sailing boat from the backseat of the automobile. "I knew I should have tried wrapping it," the lady in the hat sighed. "Hiram, bring that rug to cover it!"

Soon they were all on their way again with the birthday cake, the doctor who had to deliver the twins, the three automobile passengers and the sailboat. It was just outside town that they met a hunter carrying his lame beagle. The doctor studied the beagle's foreleg and pronounced it a bad sprain but not broken. The hunter with his dog occupied the topmost seat in the back.

When they reached the depot in Bridgewater, the platform was empty. The stationmaster was a thin man with a small beard. He was hooking a lantern to the rain gutter above the platform, since the flying snow had turned the sky gray. "Oh, I heard about the accident at the sawmill," he replied to Mr. Cady's questions. "No one hurt—just a mess on the tracks." He jumped down from the stool on which he had been standing. The lantern swayed in the wind. "But that wasn't here—that was West Bridgewater—up the line."

Dorie said, "Pa, I promise I won't be too sad if my package doesn't come 'til after Christmas."

Mr. Cady brushed the snow from his own shoulders. "We've come this far. I guess a bit farther won't matter—besides we've got these folks to deliver to the train."

"And their special Christmas package," Dorie added. She thought of the moment the one-year-old baby would set eyes on the sailboat that was a lot bigger than he was.

The Cadys dropped the doctor almost at the door of the farm he was headed for and delivered the birthday cake by way of the livery stable in Bridgewater Corners. The woman there said she knew exactly who was having the one hundredth birthday party, for it was her own great aunt, and she'd deliver the cake herself.

"There's another special Christmas package, Pa," Dorie said.

The hunter and his dog jumped out at the next side

road, and the Cadys could see smoke curling invitingly from the chimney across the river, where their farm stood back by the woods.

In Bridgewater Corners they did find the train, and it appeared the logs would be cleared before too long. In the meantime, someone had been sent over the mountain from Rutland to inspect the tracks to make sure they weren't damaged. There seemed to be every likelihood the train would reach Rutland for Christmas Eve. The travelers from Boston thanked Mr. Cady and departed with their sailboat, searching for someone to look after their automobile once the storm was over.

The Bridgewater Corners stationmaster was a white-haired man, and his office was cozy and homey, filled with souvenirs of his many years on the railroads. He insisted that the Cadys come inside and get warm while he listened to their request. "A Christmas package," he repeated, wide-eyed, when Dorie explained their mission. "You wouldn't, by any chance, be Miss Dorie Cady of Butternut Farm, would you?

Dorie jumped from her chair with surprise. "Why, yes, I am!"

"Would this be an exceedingly special Christmas

MISTLETOE MADNESS

package?" the stationmaster asked.

Mr. Cady answered for both of them: "We seem to have had a day full of extra-special Christmas packages—but I hope this one may be the best of all."

The stationmaster drew on the scarf he had just hung up by the stove. "You'd better come with me," he said. Once outside, he called to two boys shoveling the platform, "George! Francis! We'll need your help here. This young lady is Miss Dorie Cady of Butternut Farm."

The boys looked at Dorie with curiosity. "Oh," said one boy, "that's her."

Dorie and Mr. Cady followed the stationmaster to the next-to-last car. When they reached the door, the stationmaster helped Dorie up the steep steps. There—half in the hall and half in the baggage car—stood a large crate made of bright, fresh lumber. Fixed to the top was a glossy white sign that read: "My name is Trixy, and I will do my best to make a Merry Christmas for Miss Dorie Cady of Butternut Farm, Bethel, Vermont." The crate was decorated with holly and evergreen twigs. Inside, its eyes glittering back at Dorie, was a little Shetland pony with a fluffy cream forelock above its eyes and a smooth golden coat.

MISTLETOE MADNESS

"A pony! Oh, Pa!" Dorie exclaimed. "We could deliver a thousand, thousand Christmas packages and never find one as wonderful as this one!"

"Your mother said this was going to be a remarkable Christmas," Mr. Cady said happily.

"Oh, Ma was so right," Dorie exclaimed ecstatically.

"She usually is," Mr. Cady admitted.

Luise van Keuren

The Perfect Christmas Tree

The cold wind slapped me in the face. It was Christmas Eve, and my dad and I were tramping through the snow searching the woods for that perfect Christmas tree.

"Sarah, does this look like a good tree?" Dad asked, pointing at a pine tree.

I looked it over, up and down. I shook my head. "Nope. I think we can do better."

The snow crunched beneath our boots. I loved walking through the woods searching for that perfect tree, but I also missed my friends. We lived miles from anyone. I hated not being able to make friends except with the forest creatures. So I told my mom that all I wanted for

126

Christmas was a friend.

A few snowflakes drifted in the air and my feet were starting to get cold. I walked a few steps ahead of Dad. I stopped. Right in front of me stood the tallest tree covered with snow. I circled the tree, inspecting it as I shook snow from some branches. A yellow star-shaped cardboard hung from a branch. Written on the star in purple crayon, my favorite color, were the words "The perfect Christmas tree for Sarah."

"Dad, look."

Dad examined the star. "I wonder who put this there?"

"Maybe Santa." I smiled.

Dad turned the star over and over indicating he didn't know anything about it.

If Dad didn't put the star here as some kind of surprise or adventure, then who did? Out of the corner of my eye I saw something move behind a tree. I walked toward the tree. "Is someone there?"

"Sarah, is this the tree you want?" Dad asked.

I looked back at Dad. "Yeah. It looks like the perfect tree." I glanced around the woods.

"What are you doing?" Dad asked.

MISTLETOE MADNESS

"I thought I saw someone."

"Out here?"

I walked back to watch Dad chop down the tree. We hauled the tree back to the cabin. It still felt like eyes were watching us, but I didn't see anyone.

Mom had hot chocolate waiting for us. I sipped it and laughed at Dad as he tired to get the tree to stand straight. Maybe the tree wasn't so perfect, but it looked great after we got done decorating it.

"Sarah, it looks like you picked out the perfect tree," Mom said, looking the tree over.

"But I didn't really pick this tree out." I told her about the star.

A sly little smile appeared on Mom's face.

"Mom, do you know something?"

"Maybe it was Christmas angels."

Dad pulled his coat on and carried a box of lights outside. I put my coat on and followed.

Dad stood on the stepladder while I handed him the lights. The air was crisp and the stars twinkled in the clear sky.

"That should do it," Dad said, stepping down from the ladder.

MISTLETOE MADNESS

The Christmas lights blinked and twinkled in the night, competing with the stars.

"Oh, Dad, they're beautiful."

Dad stepped back to admire his work before taking the ladder inside.

I was staring at the lights when I heard a crunch of snow behind me. I turned around quickly but nothing was there.

"Anyone there?" I whispered into the dark woods. No reply.

Feeling cold, I went back inside to help Mom bake some Christmas cookies. After enjoying the Christmas tree for awhile I decided to go to bed. As I got my nightgown on I noticed it was snowing. I sat by the window. The snow began to fall, covering everything in its path. Tomorrow I could build a Christmas snowman.

Early the next morning, wrapped in my warm fuzzy robe, I slipped into the living room. My perfect Christmas tree lit up the room with a Christmasy scene. Underneath the tree Santa left piles of gifts, mostly for me. At the fireplace hung our stockings full of all kinds of goodies with a fire underneath.

"Merry Christmas, Sarah," Mom said, carrying a

platter of freshly baked cinnamon rolls. She set the plate on the table. "Let's wait a little bit before we open presents. Why don't you check out your stocking?"

"Okay," I reached for a cinnamon roll.

"Don't touch. They're still hot."

I pulled my stocking off the hook and dumped the contents onto the floor. Out rolled an apple, orange, and a lot of candy.

"Merry Christmas, Sarah," Dad said, carrying an arm full of wood into the house. He dumped it by the fireplace. "Ready to open presents?"

"Yeah."

"No. I want to wait just a little bit longer," Mom said, bringing Dad a cup of coffee. "Check out your stocking. It looks like Santa left you more than a lump of coal."

Mom and Dad looked at the items in their stockings. I had just popped a piece of candy into my mouth when there was a knock at the door.

Dad started to get up.

"Sit down." Mom motioned for Dad to sit. "Sarah, your Christmas present is at the door."

I opened the door. There stood a boy about my

age, a girl who looked about a year younger than I am and two adults behind them.

"Merry Christmas, Sarah," they said all together as if they had practiced this moment.

I stood there not believing my eyes. Will they be my friends?

"Let them in, Sarah," Mom said, standing behind me.

I stepped aside to let them enter.

They stomped snow off their boots. Mom took their coats. "It's good to see you again. Sarah, this is the new family that just moved into that old farm house."

I stood staring at them. We hadn't had guests since we moved in.

"This is my son Jeff, my daughter Amy, my wife Sue, and I'm Mike," Mike said.

Mom introduced me and Dad. "Met them in town the other day. Sarah, I told them about your wish for a friend for Christmas and they thought it would be a good idea to surprise you."

"Oh, Mom, thank you." I hugged her.

We sat around drinking hot chocolate and eating cinnamon rolls.

MISTLETOE MADNESS

Jeff strolled over to the Christmas tree and picked up the yellow star we left on the tree.

"Sarah, I see you found your perfect tree," he said.

"Did you put that there?" I asked.

He nodded.

Kay LaLone

Hannah's Christmas Ornament

Miss Lowry's class was getting ready for Christmas. All along the edge of the chalk rail, the children hung their brightly colored Christmas socks. Hannah hung her fuzzy brown woolen one at the end of the row.

Standing by the window, Laura wrinkled up her nose. She turned to her friends and said in a loud whisper, "That brown sock is ugly. It's the color of dirt. Maybe we should put a potato in it and see if it grows!" The girls burst into giggles.

Sitting in the first row, Hannah heard every word.

MISTLETOE MADNESS

Her cheeks burned. My fuzzy sock is special, she thought. Grammy knit it for me with wool from our sheep.

All afternoon, the children snipped white paper snowflakes for the bulletin boards and made colorful paper chains to hang on the Christmas tree.

"Now we need some ornaments for our tree," said Miss Lowry. Make a Christmas ornament as a gift for someone else. We'll draw numbers. On Monday, we'll put our ornaments into the socks with the matching numbers.

Laura drew first . . . number twenty-two . . . the fuzzy brown sock. "You mean I have to make something for that ugly sock?" she asked.

"Yes, Laura, you do!" said Miss Lowry. "And be kind." Laura looked away. Hannah bit the skin along the nail of her pinky finger. What would Laura make?

Hannah blinked quickly as she looked at the number she had chosen. Sock number nine was the red velvet sock, trimmed with gold braid and holly berries. Everyone knew it belonged to Laura. It was pretty and fancy—just like Laura.

I'll make her an ornament she'll never forget, thought Hannah. After school she found a piece of ragged

134

brown felt in the bottom of Grammy's scrap box. With sharp scissors she cut out the shape of a potato and glued black beads on it for eyes.

That night as Hannah and Grammy baked cookies for the class Christmas party Grammy said, "Hannah, I found a potato ornament on my sewing table today. What is it for?" Grammy listened as Hannah told the story.

"Laura was unkind when she made fun of your sock," said Grammy. "But do you really want to be unkind too?"

Hannah grumbled as she fingered through Grammy's scrap box. When she found a piece of gold felt, she cut it into the shape of a star. Then she glued round, shiny gold beads on each point. Hannah wrapped it in red tissue and stuck a bright candy cane tag on it.

On Monday morning Hannah still felt hurt. She took a potato from the refrigerator and carried it to school in her coat pocket. No one saw her drop the potato into Laura's sock. She placed the wrapped Christmas star over the top of it. Perfect, thought Hannah.

When it was time to open packages, Miss Lowry said, "We'll start with the brown sock at the end of the row."

MISTLETOE MADNESS

Hannah gave a sigh of relief as she opened her package. Inside was a jolly marshmallow snowman with a bright red scarf around his neck. Hannah smiled as she hung him on the tree.

The children all took turns opening their packages. The Christmas star twinkled and shimmered as Laura tore open the red tissue. "Thank you," said Laura, as she hung it from a bough. "It's the prettiest ornament on the tree." Then Laura felt something else in her sock. She reached way down into the toe of the sock and pulled out the potato. Everyone laughed.

"It's not funny," said Laura, blinking back her tears. The classroom became quiet. Hannah squirmed in her chair.

After the party, Miss Lowry said, "Hannah and Laura, will you please stay after school and help me take down the Christmas tree?"

Hannah began removing the paper chains, while Laura took off the lights.

In a small voice, Hannah said, "I'm sorry for being so unkind, Laura. Putting a potato in your sock was a bad joke."

"I'm sorry, too," said Laura. If I hadn't said such

mean things about your sock, none of this would have happened."

"Maybe one day you can visit our farm and watch Grammy spin wool into yarn," said Hannah.

"I'd like that."

When Hannah got home from school, she went straight to Grammy's sewing room. There on the sewing table lay the ragged felt potato ornament, just where she had left it. She hung it high up on the Christmas tree in the living room, right next to Laura's marshmallow snowman. Hannah stepped back to admire the tree. Just then the potato eyes seemed to wink as they sparkled under the tree lights.

Joanne Linden

MISTLETOE MADNESS

Illustration by Agy Wilson

A Song in the Night

"I don't want to play the chimes tonight," ten-year-old Sarah said, pulling her long dark hair back into a ponytail.

Sarah's older sister, Annie, put her hands on her hips. "What's your problem? You play the chimes every night. And tonight is Christmas Eve!"

"I just got back from seeing Mrs. Clark," Sarah sighed. "She babysat me for years, and even I can't make her smile. How do you cheer up someone who's real sick on both her birthday and Christmas Eve?"

Annie frowned. "Play something special for her on the chimes tonight. You know how she loves your music."

"I told her that would be her present," Sarah

admitted. "But I don't think her favorite carol is enough. I don't know what to do."

A thought flickered through Sarah's brain as she pulled on her winter coat. *No, I wouldn't dare*, she thought.

The squeak of the snow under her boots set Sarah's teeth on edge as she stomped down the sidewalk toward the church, pushed along by Annie. The dark sky swirled with new snowflakes.

"Are you still thinking about what to play for Mrs. Clark?" Annie asked.

"I have one idea, but . . ." Sarah said.

"What?"

"Oh, nothing. I'll hurry."

The church sat like an old man hunched over against the snow, the top of its squat tower lost in the swirling flakes. Inside, odors of candle wax and fresh greens tickled their noses as they walked toward the choir loft behind the altar, careful not to catch their heavy boots in the thin carpeting.

Part way down, Sarah stopped. *I do dare*, she thought. *But I'd better not tell Annie.*

The keyboard hummed, warming up; pages rustled

as Sarah flipped through the hymnal. Annie's voice echoed in the empty church as she urged her sister to play certain carols.

Just before six, Sarah turned on the outside speakers, holding her breath and keeping her hands away from the keyboard until her watch said exactly 5:55. Then she launched into "Silent Night." A glad smile spread over her face as she heard the high sharp sound of the chimes cutting through the snowy night outside, spreading the Christmas message. *I'm so lucky to be able to do this*, she thought.

Exactly at six o'clock, she struck the middle C note six times. She paused and then played another song, the first time anyone had played something after six o'clock. The familiar notes of "Happy Birthday" resounded through the air.

"What are you doing?" Annie cried, grabbing Sarah's left arm.

Sarah turned off the outside power. "There. What do you think?"

Wide-eyed, Annie replied, "I think you're in big trouble!" Then a grin spread over her face. "Oh, you played Happy Birthday to the Christ Child! It is his birthday!"

"Yes," Sarah grinned back. "But it also was something special for Mrs. Clark. That should make her smile!"

Lois Miner Huey

A Special Christmas Card

"But, Mother!" cried Rachel Hanson.

No buts," said her mother. "I want you to help me serve for my club meeting this afternoon and I need some help tomorrow picking up the used toys for the needy children."

"Oh, for crying out loud . . . I don't want to spend the afternoon with a bunch of old women at a club meeting!"

"That's enough, Rachel. And you will help me tomorrow."

Rachel stormed off. "I'll have to call Joey and tell him I can't work on the posters for the dance until tomorrow afternoon."

MISTLETOE MADNESS

"You have plenty of time for posters. It's still two weeks until Christmas, but we have to finish getting the toys ready."

"Toys!" Rachel snorted.

"Rachel," said her mother, quietly. "I know you have other interests, now that you're growing up. But don't forget, you liked toys only a few years ago and looked forward to Santa."

"I'm sorry, Mom," she apologized, but she was still angry about her plans. All through the meeting, Rachel was barely civil to the ladies, even though her mother kept giving her warning looks.

"How's school, Rachel?" Mrs. Dopson asked.

"Just fine, Mrs. Minnie," she answered absently.

"You certainly have grown into a fine, young lady," said the elderly woman.

"Thank you," Rachel said, a little ashamed.

After the meeting, her mother gave her a disappointed look.

"I can't help it, Mom. Mrs. Dopson gets on my nerves."

"Rachel, she is a fine person, a little funny at times, but a good friend and I would like for you to be nice to her."

"Yes, Ma'am," muttered Rachel.

The next day, Rachel was getting ready to draw the posters for the dance.

"Mom, where are those watercolor pencils Daddy used to have?"

"In the desk somewhere, I think."

Rachel's father had died a year before and his desk had never been cleaned out.

She pawed through the old papers and things, grumbling to herself.

"Good grief. Look at all this stuff." She pulled an old envelope from the bottom of a drawer.

"The postmark is five years old," she exclaimed. "Who would want to keep this?" Curiosity made her open it, though, before she chunked it aside.

It was a Christmas card. Rachel read the typed verse, and almost threw it down dismissively, when a fine script at the bottom caught her eye.

"Don't worry about the little girl's Christmas," it read, and was signed Minnie Dopson.

Rachel's mind flew back to a Christmas five years past. The flashes of conversation had not meant anything then.

"No job for awhile," she heard her father say.

"What about Christmas?" Her mother had asked.

"I don't know, I just don't know," had been the answer.

"No wonder I got so much that year," said Rachel, and her eyes filled with tears.

"Rachel, what's the matter?" Her mother asked as she walked into the room.

Rachel handed her the card.

"Oh, honey, I never meant for you to see this."

"Mom, we were broke, weren't we? And Mrs. Dopson and the club arranged for my Christmas, didn't they?"

"Yes, they did, Rachel. Your father was out of work for over three months and we just didn't have any money for Christmas."

"Mom, why didn't you tell me? I've been so hateful to Mrs. Minnie. I just thought she was a silly old lady."

"The occasion never arose to tell you, Rachel. Wouldn't it have made you feel worse knowing you had to be nice to her?"

MISTLETOE MADNESS

"I . . . I suppose so."

"Here, dry your eyes. Here comes Joey."

"Hi, Rachel, are you ready to draw up some super posters? Hey, have you been crying?"

"Not really," sniffed Rachel, "but I do have something to do before the posters are drawn."

"Now what?" Joey asked, with a sigh. He still was amazed at Rachel's moods.

"Mom, didn't I hear you say Mrs. Minnie was having some trouble with her bunions and couldn't walk to the market anymore?"

"Yes, she mentioned it the other day."

"Joey, you and I are about to take a sweet old lady, no I mean a sweet elderly lady marketing. I have an overdue debt to pay. And Mom, remind me to send Mrs. Dopson an extra special Christmas card."

"What is this all about, Rachel?" Joey asked.

Rachel blew her mother a kiss. "Come on, Joey, I think the Christmas spirit is just beginning."

Dorothy Baughman

Angie's Homemade Springtime

"It's snowing! It's snowing!" Jessie ran outside, closely followed by her older sister and mother. "That means a white Christmas, right?"

Sticking out her tongue, Angie laughed as several fluttery cold flakes found it. "Tastes like Christmas to me!" Suddenly she found her attention caught by a moving van that had pulled up across the street. Well-bundled movers opened the back and, after a small delay, began hauling out furniture.

Pushing a strand of straight brown hair behind her ear, Angie grinned at the sight of the first item, a cream-colored dresser with ivy stenciling on its side. It *could* belong to a girl her age.

However, by the time her family had finished breakfast the next morning, Angie's anticipation had turned to frustration. "But, Mom, aren't you at all curious about what kind of people are going to be living across from us?"

Mrs. Phelps, red grading pencil in hand, looked up from a stack of papers that lay on the kitchen table. "I've got just three more tests to grade and then I can enjoy Christmas vacation too. Besides, the cinnamon rolls I want to take over to them are still in the oven." She peered at Angie over half-glasses. "Why don't you go outside and see if your dad needs any help digging the car out."

Sighing, Angie grabbed her coat and plunged out the front door.

"Hey, Kiddo." Her dad looked up from shoveling. "What's up?"

"I'm here to help."

"And you sound *so* happy about it," he replied with a laugh. "Grab the scraper out of the glove box and start working on clearing the windows. I can't believe how much snow fell last night. Jessie just might get her white Christmas."

Angie got the scraper and began half-heartedly pushing piled snow off the windshield. She paused, her eyes straying to the house across the street.

Her dad noticed. "It would be nice to have a friend close by, wouldn't it, Kiddo?"

She nodded.

He took the scraper from her limp hand. "Why don't I finish up here and you go check and see if those rolls are done?"

"Thanks, Dad."

* * *

While Jessie made giant feet in the snow, Angie nervously pushed her hair behind her ear, eager to see who would answer their mother's knock.

The front door edged open, almost like the person behind it wasn't quite sure what they would find on the other side.

"Hello," Mrs. Phelps smiled at the tired-looking woman whose face finally emerged. "We're your neighbors across the street and the unofficial welcome wagon. I'm Denise Phelps and these are my daughters,

MISTLETOE MADNESS

Angie and Jessie."

"We brought cinnamon rolls," Jessie chimed in.

A small answering smile wavered around the woman's lips. "They smell wonderful." She opened the door a little wider. "Please come in. I'm Rita Dawson."

They crowded into a small entryway, made even smaller by stacks of unpacked boxes.

Mrs. Dawson beamed at Angie. "You look to be about my Raven's age. If you'd like to meet her, she's right over there in the living room. You can get acquainted while your mother and I put these rolls in the kitchen."

Angie's heart raced, but she made herself walk, not run. After all, it wouldn't be too cool to come charging around the corner like a three year old.

She paused at the door to the darkened room.

"It's all dark. Where is she?" Jessie demanded from behind.

"Well this isn't a zoo," stated a voice, "so either quit staring and come in or leave."

Startled, Angie squinted into the gloom.

"Well?"

Cautiously Angie moved forward, followed by

151

Jessie. As her eyes adjusted, she realized someone sat near an unlit fireplace. "Hello."

"Who are you?"

"Angie. I live across the street. This is my little sister, Jessie."

"We came to say hi," Jessie put in helpfully.

Angie's searching eyes found those of a girl sitting in a wheel chair, her left leg incased in a long, white cast. "I, uh, you must be Raven?"

"What happened to your leg?" Jessie asked.

The girl glared at her. "Are you always so rude?"

Lower lip trembling, Jessie pushed back behind Angie.

"She didn't mean anything by it," said Angie, "besides, refusing to give us your name is rude too."

The girl shrugged. "I didn't refuse. You just didn't give me a chance to answer. Of course I'm Raven."

Jessie pointed to the huge picture window that covered one wall. "At least you can see the snow from where you're sitting. Maybe we'll have a white Christmas."

"I HATE snow." The angry words were spat out in a hiss from between clenched teeth. "And if Christmas is going to be white, then I hate Christmas too." Suddenly, Raven's hostile face crumpled.

To Angie's surprise, the other girl looked close to tears. *Now what should I do?*

"Well, how are you girls getting along in here?" Mrs. Dawson's voice sounded loud and overly cheerful compared to the silence that had descended. "Oh my, you shouldn't be in the dark." She flipped on the lights.

Eyes blinking at the sudden light, Angie spotted her mother getting ready to go out the front door. "Uh . . ." Grabbing Jessie's arm she pushed her forward. "We've got to go now." She ignored the look of surprise that crossed her mother's face.

"Oh, yes, of course." Mrs. Dawson smiled expectantly at Angie. "I hope we'll see you back over here again soon."

"Thank you." But to herself, Angie admitted that after the way the other girl had treated Jessie, she could live without stepping a foot near Raven Dawson ever again!

After dinner Mrs. Phelps started a fire in the living room fireplace. Christmas music played softly in the background as Mr. Phelps climbed into the attic and brought down the Christmas tree that would occupy the living room for the next few weeks. Angie popped popcorn and Jessie got in everybody's way. But for once nobody minded because it was tree decorating time.

"I think," said Mrs. Phelps, "that in addition to stringing popcorn for the tree, we should make some gingerbread men ornaments to decorate it."

"Yum," agreed Jessie.

"Now remember," her dad kidded, "some of them have to go on the tree and not in your belly."

The girls just grinned.

"Angie," instructed her mother, "why don't you help me string the popcorn, while your dad and Jessie make a paper garland."

"We're making our Christmas," Jessie announced.

Her mother laughed. "I've always found that a homemade Christmas is the best kind. It's got all your love in it."

Angie and her mother settled on the floor near the fireplace.

Mrs. Phelps smiled at her oldest daughter. In a low voice, she asked, "Do you want to tell me what happened this afternoon?"

MISTLETOE MADNESS

"Raven's mean, Mom," Angie burst out in an angry whisper. "She called Jessie rude, but she was the one who was rude. All Jessie did was ask what happened to her leg." She paused to inhale.

"I see." Her mother looked thoughtful. "Mrs. Dawson told me Raven hurt her leg in a skiing accident. She's already had one surgery and will have to have another one after Christmas. She's in a lot of pain. The doctors have also told her there's a good chance that she will probably walk with a slight limp for the rest of her life."

"Oh." Angie felt a hot flush creep up her neck. "I guess that's why she seemed so upset when Jessie mentioned that we'd probably have a white Christmas."

"Possibly."

Angie suddenly felt small and miserable.

Her mother leaned over and kissed her on the top of the head, her way of dropping the subject.

Later that evening, Angie sat on her bed, knees pulled close, her chin resting on them. She loved this time of year with its bright lights, soft snow, and cheerful carols. She loved making ornaments and good things to eat . . . a "homemade Christmas" as her mother called it.

155

MISTLETOE MADNESS

But now her mind kept imagining Raven sitting in that dark living room, in pain, watching the snow that she hated come down.

It made Angie's heart hurt.

As she pondered the problem, her eyes fell on a huge tissue paper flower decorating the top of her dresser. It blazed in colors of pink, bright orange, and yellow. She'd won it at her school's spring fair. A small idea began to form in her mind. Like a seed, it took root and began to grow. Excited, Angie jumped off her bed and raced down the stairs.

"Mom, do we still have that old artificial Christmas tree that you were going to donate to charity?"

Her mother looked up from her laptop. "Yes, it's still up in the attic. Why?"

Angie grinned. "It's a surprise. Also, could you find out when Raven and her mother are going to leave their house again?"

"Mrs. Dawson said Raven has a doctor's appointment tomorrow morning. But Angie . . ."

"That's great." Angie gave her mother a hug. "Now," she said, "one last thing . . . Is there any way you could get the key to their house?"

MISTLETOE MADNESS

"Maybe . . . but, Angie . . ."

Angie took a deep breath. She explained to her mother exactly what she had in mind.

"Oh, Angie," her mother said softly when she'd finished. "That's a wonderful idea."

Angie spent the rest of the evening working in her room.

"Whatcha doing?" Jessie asked, as she and her teddy bear were getting ready for bed.

Angie told her.

Jessie's eyes widened. "I want to help."

"Okay, you can make a picture."

"Of what?"

"Anything you want."

The next day Angie felt jumpy, until she saw the Dawson's car finally leave the driveway. Then she and Jessie carried all the necessary items over to their new neighbors' house.

Last of all, Mr. Phelps placed the old tree beside the living room fireplace. Before he left he gave her a big hug. "I'm proud of you, Angie."

A little embarrassed, she just shrugged her shoulders and grinned.

MISTLETOE MADNESS

The sisters worked hard. Several times Angie felt frustration rising as she tried to get an item "just right." Finally, the last piece of the plan, Jessie's artwork, went up.

Just in time, too. A car had pulled into the driveway. Behind it they could see their parents hurrying over from across the street.

Angie's stomach rolled as thousands of butterflies came alive inside of it. "Come on," she told Jessie, "let's go stand by the couch so she sees the room first."

Pushed by her mother, Raven entered the room. Her eyes grew wide.

Nervously, Angie tried to see the room as the other girl might be seeing it.

On the tree, soft white lights twinkled amid ribbons of pink, green, yellow, and blue. At its very top, instead of an angel or a star, hung Angie's summer straw hat. Its rim of white flowers made a pretty halo effect. Her big tissue paper flower occupied the very center of the fireplace mantle. A carefully assembled pink and green construction paper chain hung like swag off the edge. Under the tree lay a white felt tree skirt covered in glitter. Piled on it were all the stuffed animals she and Jessie could scrounge from their rooms.

"Happy Homemade Springtime," Angie softly told Raven.

Raven turned to stare at her. "You . . . you did this?"

Angie nodded.

"Even after I was so mean to you?"

Angie shrugged.

"I helped," Jessie spoke up. She ran over to the picture window and pointed. "This is mine."

The large, slightly lopsided yellow sun with its cheery smiling face almost covered the big window.

"If you don't feel like seeing snow, you can look at it and pretend it's sunny."

"It's beautiful," Raven whispered. She swallowed. "Thank you. I . . . I still can't believe you did something so nice."

Angie looked at Mrs. Dawson. Raven's mother had tears running down her cheeks. "Thank you," she said.

As they walked home, Angie's mother hugged her. "I'm so proud of you, sweetie. You remembered that the true meaning of Christmas is giving."

MISTLETOE MADNESS

"Even," said her father with a grin, "if you had to visit springtime to do it!"

Susan Meyers

MISTLETOE MADNESS

Illustration by Regina Kubelka

The Good Old Days

"Hurray!" Nick shouted when he looked out the window. "They're starting the snow machines tonight."

"Hmph," said Nick's grandpa.

Nick sighed. He knew he was going to hear all about how snow should be real instead of plastic and people should do their holiday shopping at stores instead of on computers. Grandpa had come to spend Christmas with Nick.

Nick loved his grandfather, but sometimes he got tired of hearing about the "good old days." This *was* the twenty-second century after all, and things were a lot better now. This morning he had video-mails on his computer from each of his friends showing him what presents they had picked out for themselves—from him. He and his dad had already exchanged Christmas certificates because his dad would be away on a business trip for the next two weeks.

Nick's dad thought it was a good idea if Grandpa came to stay for a while. "Your Grandpa gets lonely sometimes," Nick's dad had said. But Nick didn't need the company. He wasn't a little kid who had to have someone watching him all the time. Besides, he had Sam—his robot.

Sam was Nick's "Security and Maintenance" robot. He made sure all the machines in the house worked right—especially Nick's favorite machine, the food dispenser. Nick's magneticar always ran, thanks to Sam. Life was just easier with a robot. Not according to Grandpa, though.

"Stupid machines all over the place. Nobody does anything by themselves anymore," was what Nick heard from Grandpa all the time.

"I don't know what present I can give Grandpa that would make him happy," Nick told Sam that night as they turned off the daytime machines.

"What does he like to do?" Sam asked.

MISTLETOE MADNESS

"He likes to build things."

"What kind of things?"

"Houses," Nick said.

"Houses?" Sam asked. "Houses come already assembled."

"Not in the good old days," Nick said. "Grandpa used to build houses. Now machines build houses. Grandpa hates machines." Nick's face turned red. "Oops, sorry Sam."

Sam shook his metal head. "No problem."

"It is for me," said Nick. What could he possibly give Grandpa as a Christmas present? Everything he thought of would just make Grandpa grumble about the good old days.

The next day was Christmas Eve. When Nick woke up, the house felt colder than usual. It seemed that the heat had gone off early in the morning.

"Beautiful morning, isn't it?" Grandpa greeted Nick in the kitchen.

"It's cold. And I can't get the food dispenser to work," Nick grumbled.

"Or the sunlight simulator. Or the electronic doors," Grandpa said with a smile. "All the machines have stopped working."

"Where's Sam?" Nick looked for his robot and found him standing in the hallway. He was as still as a refrigerator. No matter how many screws Nick turned or how many buttons he pushed, the robot wouldn't move.

"But what are we going to eat? How are we going to keep warm?" Nick asked.

"We'll have to make our own heat. Cook our own food," Grandpa said. "First we need to build a stove."

"But we need machines to do that . . ."

Grandpa frowned. "Nonsense. People have been taking care of themselves for thousands of years, Nick. We can live without machines."

"Okay, well . . ." Nick thought for a minute. "Lisa builds fires when she goes camping on Venus."

"Who's Lisa? She sounds like a smart girl."

"She's a friend of mine who lives next door. She and her mom went to her grandmother's house on Mars for the holidays," Nick said. "She won't mind if we borrow some of her camping stuff. She keeps it in her garage."

"Wonderful," Grandpa said. "Let's go on a scavenger hunt!"

MISTLETOE MADNESS

Nick didn't know what that meant, but Grandpa made it sound like fun.

And it was! They dragged home a small wood-burning stove, cans and boxes of food, and some candles.

Grandpa opened a vent in the ceiling, then set up a campfire right in the middle of the living room. They warmed up two cans of soup while they munched on crackers smeared with peanut butter and jelly.

"Wow," Nick said. "I choose this all the time from the food dispenser but it never tastes like this! Is this what food tasted like in the good old days?"

After they ate they put on lots of sweaters—one on top of the other—and read stories to each other from an adventure book Grandpa had brought. Grandpa showed Nick how to play games with a pack of cards he had packed in his luggage. "This is called poker," Grandpa said.

"I thought polka was something people used to dance to." Nick said and Grandpa laughed and laughed. The day went faster than any day Nick could remember.

When it was time to go to sleep, Nick hugged Grandpa. "This has been a great Christmas, hasn't it?"

"The best ever," Grandpa said and hugged Nick

MISTLETOE MADNESS

back.

Later that night, after Grandpa was asleep, Nick took a little metal piece from under his pillow and snuck into the hallway where Sam stood frozen. He opened a flap on Sam's back and stuck the metal piece into him. Sam began to hum and buzz. His lights flashed and then slowed to a steady brightness.

"How did it go?" he asked Nick.

"Great! Grandpa had a terrific Christmas."

"That was a nice present you gave him," Sam said.

Nick smiled and ran back to bed.

L.C. Mohr

Jordan's Shoes

"But, Mom!" Jordan followed his mother into the kitchen. "I've got to have those tennis shoes."

"How many times must I say no?" Mom opened the oven and took out an apple pie.

"But everybody has them," Jordan said. "The kids call me 'Generic' because of my dumb-looking shoes."

Mom set the pie beside a pot of stew. "You already have two pairs of perfectly good tennis shoes."

"I promise I'll never ask for another thing, if you'll buy me those shoes."

"That's what you said about the skateboard, and the roller blades, and the video games." She started loading two paper sacks with food.

"What if I pay for them myself?"

Mom shook her head. "Even if you had a hundred dollars, I wouldn't let you waste your money."

"What if it's the only Christmas present you get for me this year?" He just *had* to fit in with the other kids at school.

"We've already bought your Christmas present." She put the apple pie into a plastic container with a handle.

"But, Mom—"

"No! No more." She nodded to the overflowing garbage can. "Please take out the trash, and then you can help me deliver this food."

Jordan sighed as he picked up the can and took it to the garage. Why couldn't Mom understand? The kids with cool brands of tennis shoes teased him about his "generic" shoes. It wasn't fair! And now he had to help take food to some family across town. Why didn't they buy their own?

As he dumped the trash into the large can, Jordan thought about the money he'd saved to buy Christmas gifts. Counting the pennies in his change jar, he had about forty-seven dollars. Sometimes Grandma and Aunt Sandi gave him money for Christmas. Maybe he could save it all and do some extra chores.

Maybe he'd better start acting cheerful about helping. He closed the trash can and ran back inside to wash his hands.

"I'm ready, Mom," he said, as cheerfully as he could. "What can I carry?"

"Well," she said, smiling. "Those words are music to my ears."

Jordan groaned as he took one of the bags from her. Mom sure could be corny.

The radio played "Rudolph, the Red-Nosed Reindeer," while they drove to a part of town that Jordan had never seen before. He kept looking down at the stew in the pot between his feet, afraid that it would slosh out on his tennis shoes.

"How did you find out about this family, anyway?" he asked.

"Your Aunt Sandi told me about the Smiths. They have seven children."

"Seven?" One older sister was enough for Jordan. "You didn't tell me that part!"

"They live in a two bedroom house with a broken

stove, so they can't cook anything."

What could you eat that didn't need to be cooked? Cold cereal? Peanut butter and jelly sandwiches?

"Here we are." His mother pulled up to a small wooden house with a bare dirt yard. A rusty tricycle lay on its side near the street.

"I don't understand, Mom," Jordan said. "Did they ask you to bring food?"

She shook her head. "The agency Aunt Sandi works for is helping them buy a new stove, but she and I felt badly that they were having such a hard time at Christmas."

"Can't they buy their own stove?" Jordan asked.

"Mr. Smith is in the hospital. Mrs. Smith has no money for a sitter, so she isn't working, either." She handed Jordan one of the sacks while she carried the stew pot. They went up the rickety steps to the front porch.

"Will you please knock, Jordan?"

Before Jordan could figure out how to knock on the torn screen door, a little girl opened the wooden door behind it and squealed.

"Mama!" she cried. "Somebody's here!"

A tired-looking woman holding a baby on her hip

came to the door.

"I'm Myra Daniels," Jordan's mother said. "My sister, Sandi Ryan, told me about your stove. We brought you a hot meal."

"I know Mrs. Ryan," said Mrs. Smith. "Come in."

Jordan followed his mother inside. Several children crowded behind Mrs. Smith. The whole house was clean, but everything in it was old and worn out. Unlike his house, which was decorated for Christmas with a real pine tree and lights on the windows, the Smiths had a lopsided plastic tree on a table decorated with homemade paper ornaments. There were no presents under the tree.

A boy Jordan's age stepped into the room. "Who's here, Mom?" The boy stared at Jordan.

"Brian, this is Mrs. Daniels," said Mrs. Smith.

"Hi, I'm Jordan," he said without being asked. "There's another bag. You want to come with me and get it?"

Brian shrugged and followed Jordan to the car. Jordan picked up the grocery bag, and a can of fruit cocktail fell out. Brian grabbed it before it rolled into the street.

"I'm in seventh grade," said Jordan.

"Me, too," Brian said.

"I go to McAuliffe Middle School."

"So do I. I've seen you around."

"You have?" Jordan couldn't remember ever seeing Brian.

"You have a nice car," said Brian.

"Thanks." Jordan noticed there was no car in Brian's gravel driveway.

Then Jordan looked down at Brian's feet. He wore generic tennis shoes, too. But his were so worn that Jordan could see skin through the holes. The shoelaces had broken off, so the tongues flopped around when Brian walked.

Jordan hoped Brian wouldn't look too closely at his own shoes. There were no holes in them. His new shoelaces shone bright white.

Jordan's mother helped Mrs. Smith empty the grocery bags.

"This is so nice of you," said Mrs. Smith.

"I'm glad we could help. I hope your husband gets well real soon." Jordan's mom said as she headed toward the car.

"Hey, Brian," Jordan said. "Maybe I'll see you at school."

"Yeah." Brian stuck his hands in his pockets.

"Merry Christmas," said Mrs. Smith.

As they drove away, Jordan had an idea. He just hoped Mom wouldn't say it was too close to Christmas and that they were too busy.

"Mom, could I give Brian my other tennis shoes? I've only worn them a couple of times."

She looked at him.

"I want to buy the other kids something with my Christmas money, maybe a new tricycle. And they really need some nicer ornaments for that poor little tree. Could we go back before Christmas? Please?"

"Sure, Jordan," Mom said, smiling. "We sure can."

Catherine Jones

Janet's Christmas Candle

Janet read the directions in her second grade Weekly Reader which had arrived a few days earlier:

Easy-to-Make Lost Wax Candle

Assemble supplies: 20" of heavy string for wick, pencil, one pound of paraffin, two or three candle stubs for desired color, one tray of ice cubes, one empty quart-sized milk carton, scissors or sharp knife, one old pot for melting paraffin.

Janet could just see the smile on her mother's face

when she would unwrap her very own Christmas candle like the one shown in the picture.

When her mother left to attend a PTA meeting at school the next evening, Janet knew this was the chance she was hoping for. As the meetings were usually over in an hour or so, Janet knew she would have to hurry. Her father, who was reading the newspaper in the den, barely looked up when Janet announced she was going to be busy making a gift for her mother.

Feeling very grown up at the moment, Janet tied a pretty embroidered apron around her waist and began the project.

While the wax, bought the day before with money she had been saving from her allowance, was melting, Janet found two short red candles in the dining room buffet and added them to the pot. Then she painstakingly began following the step-by-step instructions:

Cut top off empty milk carton and rinse
it thoroughly. Knot one end of string
around a pencil. Position the pencil
across the top of the carton so the string
will form a wick.

It seemed to take a long time for the wax to melt, but finally it looked ready. Next Janet read:

Spread old newspaper on a table or counter. Fill milk carton to the top with ice cubes. Now, using care, pour melted wax into the carton. As ice cubes begin to melt, gradually add more paraffin until milk carton is full.

Pouring the remaining wax from the pot into the sink, she followed the words of the last paragraph:

Wait for candle to completely harden. Cut string to wick length. Carefully tear away carton to reveal the candle.

In Janet's eyes, the reddish-pink candle on the kitchen counter was even more beautiful than the one in the picture. She could hardly wait for the time when it would illuminate their dining room table. Carefully wrapping the candle in the wrapper saved from a loaf of bread, Janet tiptoed past her father's chair and hid the artistic creation in the back of her closet where it would stay until Christmas day.

While cleaning up the clutter in the kitchen, Janet made a horrible discovery. The leftover wax had hardened in the sink drain! She knew her father would be furious if he had to call a plumber. Janet decided the only thing to do was to try to unstop the sink herself. She had heard her mother talk about how people always boiled water whenever there was an emergency. So, drawing from this knowledge, she filled a pot of water and put it on the stove.

"Dear God, please let this work before Daddy finds out, and before mother gets home," Janet prayed, as she poured the boiling water into the drain. The hot water softened the top of the wax enough so that by sticking a turning fork down into the drain, she was able to remove the three-inch-long plug of wax. Then Janet boiled another pot of water and poured it into the sink. As she watched the water drain out freely, she mumbled, "Thank you, God, thank you."

Satisfied she was leaving the kitchen in good order, Janet again tiptoed past her father, went into her bedroom and got ready for bed.

MISTLETOE MADNESS

Not quite asleep when her mother returned home, Janet listened with particular attention when she asked if everything had been okay while she was gone. Her father said it had, and then to Janet's surprise added, "Well, honey, I learned one thing about our daughter tonight. I know for certain she believes in God."

"Why's that?" her mother asked.

"Because while you were gone, she was doing something out in the kitchen and a couple of times I heard her praying," was his reply.

Carol J. Rhodes

MISTLETOE MADNESS

Illustration by Elsbet Vance

The Great
Christmas Tree Caper

"This will look great at the nursing home," Dad said as we watched the small cedar crash to the ground. Dad, Priscilla, and I dragged the tree to the truck and tossed it in.

Once inside the truck, I blew warm air into my hands.

"Do I have to go to the nursing home, Dad? It's BOR-ING!"

"Yes, son, those people love to see Gabby."

"Gabby's the hit of any party," said Pris, my sister, brushing her bangs out of her eyes.

181

MISTLETOE MADNESS

I had to smile. Gabby is my black-and-white cat with the yellow moon eyes and the fiercest growl this side of Big Cat Ranch.

"But Dad, those people don't like Gabby. No one ever smiles when we bring him."

"No more discussion. You will be going, son. Besides, we'll be singing carols and reading the Christmas story," said Dad.

Later that day, at the nursing home, I gazed out the picture window. Snowflakes dotted the yard. Reluctantly, I helped Dad set up the tree. We decorated it with gold and red balls.

BOR-ING. Mom added some of our favorite ornaments, including a ceramic angel, some crocheted hearts, and a couple of bells. Then Dad, Pris, and I draped silver tinsel on it. *Hmmm, it doesn't look too bad*, I thought.

My Sunday School class gathered around the piano and we watched Mom set up her music. Pris sat in a chair blowing bubbles with her purple Bubbly-Bubbly bubble gum.

Some grandmas and grandpas sat against the wall in wheelchairs. Others fidgeted in their rooms ready for

MISTLETOE MADNESS

the action to begin. "Come on, let's go bring them in!" I shouted to a couple of kids. I pushed a gray-haired lady in her wheelchair, and said, "Let's go listen to some Christmas music."

One by one, we helped people into the dining room. I was proud of our beautiful Christmas tree with colorful blinking lights, but no one seemed to notice. They all seemed sad.

Miss Goosie, who sat in a corner chair fiddling with her blanket, seemed mad at the world.

When we'd brought Gabby to the nursing home before, people had barely noticed. I'm talking about a cat with attitude! And nobody noticed. I remember taking a straw from a juice glass and tossing it on the floor.

"Get it, Gabby!" Gabby skidded like a marble on a waxed floor. Then he picked up the straw, arched his back and pranced back, dropping the straw at my feet.

I waited for applause, but no one clapped. No one smiled. No one even paid attention. *Lord,* I prayed, *please don't let this day be boring.*

Joey and Jamie served chocolate chip cookies. Other kids sang off-tune Christmas carols. By the time I sat down, Pris had started reading the story of Jesus' birth.

183

"An angel of the Lord appeared to them," she said, "and the glory of the Lord shone around them, and they were . . ." she stopped a moment. Panic grew in her eyes.

". . . terrified!" she said, pointing toward the tree.

I turned to see a ball of black-and-white fur racing toward the tree.

"Oh no! Don't, Gabby!" But I was too late. Gabby scrambled up that tree like a dog after a 'coon! He batted gold and red glass balls all over the place. KER-RASH! One splatted on the freshly waxed floor. KER-RASH! Another splat!

Miss Goosie looked up from her lap. Her scowl was gone. She grinned.

"Get outta there, Gabby!" I shouted, racing toward the tree. Gabby let out an ear-splitting caterwaul and lurched into the branches, knocking down ornaments.

"Mrrooow," Gabby snarled as I yanked him out of the tree. Gabby's black tail was pumped up and his eyes looked as big as two moons.

I tried to calm him down. "Come on, Gabby, let's go find a mouse or something."

Heading into the kitchen, I tripped over a throw rug and dropped Gabby. I grabbed for Gabby's black tail, but missed. Within seconds, Gabby was back! Straight up the tree! Climbing and clawing. He wrestled something inside the tree. Small branches snapped and popped as Gabby forged upward.

Soon, Gabby jumped down from the tree with a limp, black rag hanging from his mouth. When the rag squealed, Mom screamed. Loud! Gabby looked up with innocent yellow eyes and dropped his quarry. In a second, the thing was airborne.

It looked as though it was headed for Miss Goosie's gray hair and she screamed. It was the liveliest I'd ever seen her. Then it glided back to the tree.

Gabby leapt onto the tree again. The tree lurched from side to side. More balls crashed to the floor mingling with a carpet of tinsel. Just as the tree smashed to the floor, my cat emerged grinning from ear to ear with . . . A BAT!

A bat! Horror of horrors! In the nursing home. My name was worse than mud. "Pris, read!" I shouted. Right before she began to read, I noticed that a man who was sitting near a window laughed out loud. Giggles came from some of the ladies.

I hated bats! I sucked up my courage and dove for

Gabby, who turned loose of the bat, which, in turn, glided innocently into an open utility closet.

Pris blew one monstrous bubble with her purple bubble gum and it burst—all over her face.

"Read, Pris, please read!" I pleaded, trying to distract everyone from the bat and the cat incident.

Picking the purple Bubbly-Bubbly gum off her face, Pris said, "Do not be afraid. I bring you good news of great joy that will be for all the people."

"Great joy!" echoed Miss Goosie, clapping her hands. "I haven't had this much fun in years."

Pris continued. "Today in the town of David a Savior has been born to you; he is Christ the Lord."

I crept up to the utility closet and peered in. I pulled a string attached to a light bulb. The place lit up like a firecracker. I searched the room from top to bottom. I tossed out a couple of wastebaskets, a broom, a mop, and all kinds of cleaning stuff. But there was no bat.

I crawled onto the stepladder to get a better look, when something black-and-white flashed in front of my eyes. *I'm dying!* I thought. *My life just flashed before my eyes!* Just then, Gabby cornered the bat. I grabbed the wastebasket and WHOMP! I plopped it upside-down over the bat.

"I'm sorry," I said to the nursing home director. "The bat's in the closet. I'm so sorry. . ."

"Look at them!" the man interrupted. "They're all smiling. Don't worry about the mess; we'll take care of it later. Just make these people happy."

"Go ahead, Pris," I said, "finish reading."

Pris pulled some more bubble gum from her chin and stuck it in her mouth. "This will be a sign to you: You will find a baby wrapped in cloths and lying in a manger."

I looked around the room at all the grandparents. Each had a look of pure joy. Miss Goosie was still grinning.

"Suddenly a great company of the heavenly host appeared with the angel, praising God and saying, 'Glory to God in the highest, and on earth peace to men on whom his favor rests.'"

Later, I sat on the floor listening to Miss Goosie and the others sing about Jesus, and I felt His favor resting on me, too. I knew that Jesus made His presence known in the nursing home that day—and it wasn't even BORING.

Nanette Thorsen-Snipes

Mary Lynn Learns
a Lesson in Patience

Mary Lynn's eyes opened wide when she heard the sound of a leaf blower outside her bedroom window. She jumped out of bed and peeked through the blinds. The sun was shining brightly, and seeing her father without his jacket on told her the weather would be like yesterday had been—unusually warm for mid-December.

Suddenly she remembered it was Saturday, the day of the Sunday School Christmas party. All the children of the church were invited to arrive at three o'clock in the afternoon. Each was to bring a wrapped present for the gift exchange. Mary Lynn remembered the day she and her mother had spent more than an hour in Lloyd's Department Store selecting just right gift for her to take, a gold-colored bracelet with a brilliant green stone in the center.

Mary Lynn dressed quickly and dashed downstairs for breakfast. After helping her mother with the dishes, she asked, "What time is it?"

"Oh, I don't know," her mother replied. "Go look at the clock in the bedroom."

Mary Lynn went into the bedroom and looked at the large wind-up clock on her father's dresser. The hands showed it was only five minutes to nine.

When Mary Lynn returned to the kitchen, her father was just finishing a cup of coffee. "Have to hurry or I'll be late for my golf game. I'll be home around supper time."

Mary Lynn followed her father outside and waved as he backed the car out of the driveway. Hurrying back into the house, she said, "Mother, guess what? It's so nice and warm I won't have to wear a sweater to the party today."

"Well, we'll have to see about that when it's time to go," her mother responded.

MISTLETOE MADNESS

For a few minutes, Mary Lynn played in the living room with her kitten, Muff, then went into the kitchen where her mother was ironing. "Mother, is it time for me to start getting dressed yet?"

"I don't think so, but go look at the clock and see what time it is."

Mary Lynn went into the bedroom and looked at the clock. The hands read twenty minutes to ten. Over and over that morning she asked her mother what time it was, and she would reply, "I don't know, what does the clock say?" To a six-year-old, it seemed it would never be time to go to the party.

When it was eleven o'clock, Mary Lynn decided the best way to make the time pass faster was to simply move the clock's hands ahead. Every so often she would go into the bedroom and move the hands forward, sometimes by as much as twenty or thirty minutes.

Finally, when Mary Lynn announced to her mother that the hands on the clock read two o'clock, her mother agreed it was time to get ready.

A green and red plaid taffeta dress trimmed in black velvet, made by her mother especially for the occasion, was pressed and hanging on the door of Mary

MISTLETOE MADNESS

Lynn's closet. New patent leather slippers and shiny red hair ribbons would complete her total look.

Mary Lynn's mother surely must have known it was nowhere near the appointed time for the party, but if she did, she never let on. She helped Mary Lynn with the zipper of her dress and brushed her long blonde curls. As they went out of the door, her mother gave Mary Lynn's hair bows a final touch and told her how pretty she looked.

It was only a ten-minute drive to the church and, of course, when Mary Lynn and her mother arrived, no one else was there. Still not wanting her mother to know she had set the clock ahead, Mary Lynn did not protest when her mother said, "Well, it looks like you're a little early. Just go ahead and wait on the steps. The others should be getting here soon."

Just as Mary Lynn was about to open the car door, Mrs. Holt, the church organist, pulled her car into the parking lot. Mary Lynn's mother went over and spoke briefly with her, after which Mrs. Holt said, "Come on, Mary Lynn. You can wait with me until the other children get here. I have to practice the music for my recital next Sunday, and I'll be glad to have you as my audience."

MISTLETOE MADNESS

Mary Lynn glanced over her shoulder as her mother drove off, then followed Mrs. Holt into the church. Two hours passed before the others arrived for the party where they found Mary Lynn asleep on a pew. Her new dress was wrinkled and one of her hair bows had come untied.

Carol J. Rhodes

The Marshall Family:
The Mystery of the Missing Christmas Ornaments

It is the first of December and the city streets are hanging thick with Christmas decorations. The department store is offering horse-drawn carriage rides to get us in the Christmas spirit and Christmas music fills the air.

Let me introduce you to our family. We are the Marshall family. There are five of us: Dad and Mom and three boys, John, James (we call him Jimmy), and me, Jason.

I am the one in the middle. I'm not the youngest or

193

MISTLETOE MADNESS

the oldest, just stuck in between. We drew straws to see who would tell our story and this time I was the winner. Boy, am I glad! It was getting a little crazy around here with Christmas coming, so now I can have some fun.

For a little background, let me tell you a few things about us. We live in a city of about 100,000 people in the state of Oregon.

My dad is a computer programmer and works for a big company about thirty minutes away from our home. He works a lot, but always makes time for playing baseball, or eating pizza, or riding bikes.

My mom stays at home and works to keep the house clean and all of our schedules straight. I really like to come home from school and have milk and warm cookies waiting for me at the kitchen table.

My oldest brother is John. He just turned twelve, so he is starting to act a little weird. You know, he acts normal sometimes, like a kid, and then he starts acting like an adult, and doesn't have time to play with Jimmy and me. John is still a good older brother. He is really good at math, and he helps me with my homework if I have a tough problem.

Then, there is me, Jason. I am nine years old and

stuck right in the middle. They say I'm the quiet one. I don't have much choice when I have a big brother and a little brother who want lots of attention from Mom and Dad. I really like to go fishing with Grandpa Marshall. We go to the river and hang out together. We even catch a fish once and a while.

My younger brother is James. We call him Jimmy. James sounds too grown up for my little brother. He is six years old. Jimmy is very active. He is good at all the sports, but likes baseball the best. One of his other favorite games is to pretend he is a spy. He is good at it, too, so you have to watch out if you are trying to keep a secret. Jimmy is everywhere!

The other two main characters of our family in this story are Grandpa and Grandma Marshall. These are my dad's parents. They live about one hour from the city. Their house is old and has lots of secret places to play. They have a fish pond, an old barn filled with treasures, and lots of land to run on.

Grandpa and Grandma Marshall are snowbirds. No, they don't have wings and fly. During the winter, they leave their home in the Pacific Northwest and they go to their second home in Arizona. Grandpa says that the cold

MISTLETOE MADNESS

weather makes his bones ache, so the dry, hot weather is just perfect for him.

The good news is that we just got a letter from Grandma Marshall and our family is invited to spend Christmas vacation at our grandparents' house in the country, even though they won't be there. Grandpa and Grandma Marshall left the day after Thanksgiving and will be enjoying a sunny Christmas in Arizona.

Mom says that we will leave the city on December 22nd, which is the day after the Christmas program at church. Before we go, we have to buy Christmas presents, and pack our clothes, and make sure we have our lines memorized. It's really embarrassing when you forget what you are supposed to say when five hundred people are watching.

I'm going to give you the highlights of the next three weeks and then get to the good part about our trip to the country. Here is the short version of the story. John made all his Christmas presents, but won't tell us what they are. He got an A on his math test and he is going to help Dad load the car.

Jimmy has been bouncing all over the house with excitement. He helped Mom decorate the Christmas cookies. They look really good, even if Jimmy did end up with red and green sprinkles all over his shirt. Mom helped Jimmy with his presents for all of us, so I think I'll get something good from him. Jimmy's job before we leave is to make sure all the lights are turned off in the house.

Dad has been really busy at work with Christmas deadlines. One night when I woke up to get a glass of water, I heard him down in his workshop really late. I wonder what special surprise he has for us this year. Dad asked me to remind him to fill the gas tank before we leave the city. They don't have very many gas stations out in the country where Grandpa and Grandma live.

Mom has been baking day and night. There are lots of Christmas presents under the tree, but we are not supposed to peek. I noticed that there is a big green box with my name on it. I wonder what it could be. Mom asked me to remind her to take all the Christmas snacks from the refrigerator and freezer before we go to the country. I won't forget about the food; that's one of my favorite parts of Christmas.

What have I been doing? I finished my book report and turned it in. I bought my family's Christmas presents

MISTLETOE MADNESS

at the Dollar Store, and I almost finished the pictures that I have drawn for each of them. I bought a present for my best friend, Henry. He likes to read, so I got him a new book by his favorite author.

It is now December 22nd and we are moments away from leaving. Dad and John are packing the car. Dad filled the gas tank before they started. Mom has put all the food in the ice chest for our trip. Jimmy has started turning the lights out in the house and I made sure we have the bag of games to play on the way to Grandma and Grandpa's house.

Finally, we are on our way. As we travel along it begins to snow. We will be safe, though, since Dad put the snow tires on, just in case. I still remember one winter when we got stuck in a snowdrift as we hit that first hill. Dad was not a happy camper!

It seems like we just left home, and we have already arrived. The yard is covered with a sprinkling of snow that looks like powdered sugar. We all help bring our luggage in, plus the presents and the food. Wow, I'm tired.

Mom asked, "Kids, do you want some dinner before you get settled in?"

MISTLETOE MADNESS

"Sure," we replied in unison. We all gathered around the kitchen table as Mom put out plates of homemade rolls with ham and cheese, potato chips, juice, and angel cookies, my favorite.

As we ate our food, we talked about our plans for the next day. "I want to play in the snow," said Jimmy. "Let's play in the barn," replied John. Mom and Dad discussed our plans a little longer.

"I will go to the woods and find a Christmas tree for the living room. I need all of you to help your Mother find the decorations and be ready to start when I return," said Dad.

We agreed that this was a good plan. But where would we start? Mom said, "Let's worry about that tomorrow. It's getting late and we still need to make your beds before bedtime."

The night was quiet as the snow silently drifted downward. Mom and Dad sat by the fireplace enjoying some time together after we finally made it to bed. My dreams were filled with presents and stockings, Christmas trees and snowmen.

As I rolled over, the sun was shining through the window. I hopped out of bed and looked to see how much it had snowed. There was about a foot of snow on the ground. Perfect for making snowmen, but a little rough for Dad to tromp through the woods.

After a great breakfast of waffles and eggs with Grandma's homemade maple syrup, we thought we would start looking for the decorations. "Wait a minute," Mom said as she left the sink, "Grandma left you a note; let's see what it says."

Since John is the oldest, he got to read the note. This is what it said:

"John, Jason, and Jimmy, Welcome to our home! Sorry we can't join you for the Christmas holiday, but we would really appreciate if you would decorate the house. I hate to see a house without decorations at Christmas. There is only one problem. I didn't have time to get the decorations out for you. So, I thought we could make a little game out of it. Think of it as a treasure hunt. I will give you three clues to help you find the decorations. I know you are very smart boys, so it will be no problem for you. Here is the first clue: I remember I put the Christmas ornaments in a place that's warm and dry. There are three boxes—red, green, and blue, like the sky. The next clue you will find where Grandpa spends most of his time. It's a place he can sit and watch the sunshine."

We talked it over and came up with a couple of ideas—the garden, the kitchen, or the front porch. "We are here in the kitchen already and I don't see another note, so I don't think this is the right place," I said. There were two other places to explore, the garden and the front porch.

I volunteered to take Jimmy with me and we would look at the front porch. John headed out to the garden to look around. Hopefully, Grandma had put the note somewhere that wasn't buried in the snow.

Jimmy and I went to the front porch. The front porch is enclosed so you can sit and look out on the yard without having the rain or snow fall on you. Grandpa likes to sit out there and read, and take a nap (it's our little secret). Grandma sits out there in the rocking chair and crochets or just listens to the sounds of the birds or other animals passing by.

Jimmy let out a shriek, "I found it! I found it!" I went over to Jimmy and found another one of Grandma's envelopes with her writing on it. Grandma told me once that she got an "A" in penmanship. They called it cursive writing when Grandma was growing up.

MISTLETOE MADNESS

I called out to John and he came running up to the porch. We sat down on the chairs to read the note. This time it was my turn, so I carefully opened the envelope.

"Boys, congratulations, you found the second clue! So glad you made it this far, the next place you need to look is Grandpa's old car. It's in the old barn, just fifty steps from here, and when you get there, don't forget to check out the mirror."

We had put on our coats and boots before we began our treasure hunt, so we all ran to the barn. Since the snow was deep, we decided the best way was to put Jimmy between me and John, and then if the snow was too deep, we could swing him ahead one step at a time.

When we got to the barn, we had to dig some of the snow away with our hands. It took all three of us to pull the door open, but nothing was going to stop us now. It was warm and dry when we opened the door and there were lots of places to play and treasures galore.

As we walked across the floor, we saw an old bike, and the wheelbarrow and rake from Grandpa's garden chores. There were many things that grabbed our attention, but we had to find Grandpa's old car.

We turned the corner and there was Grandpa's old

MISTLETOE MADNESS

Model T. It was his greatest treasure, so we were always very careful when he let us look at it. On the rearview mirror, there was a note from Grandma.

Since John was the tallest, we let him get the envelope for us. Jimmy doesn't read big words very well yet, so we voted to let John read the clue from Grandma.

"Congratulations! Your hunt is almost finished. The three boxes of decorations you are looking for are just a math problem away. First, multiply four times ten, and walk that many steps toward the old tractor straight ahead. Second, when you get to the tractor, you'll see the wagon is still attached. Go to the back tire on the right side and you will find directions to the packages."

We quickly did the math, and agreed that four times ten was forty, so quickly paced off forty steps. We went to the wagon wheel on the right-hand side in the back and found an envelope.

We let Jimmy open the envelope and inside was a key. There was a note from Grandma, and I got to read it this time, "Go back to the house and you will find a closet under the main staircase as you enter the front door. The key unlocks the closet and you will find the ornaments to decorate the Christmas tree and the house."

203

MISTLETOE MADNESS

We all ran back to the house, stumbling and falling in our excitement, but we made it to the house, looking like three snowmen ourselves.

We shook off the snow before we went inside. Mom had hot chocolate and warm chocolate chip cookies fresh from the oven. We told Mom we would be right back, since we had found the location of the decorations.

Through the kitchen and living room and into the front hall, we scurried on our way. We walked straight ahead and there, under the stairs, was a door just as Grandma said. John opened the door and inside the closet we found the red, green, and blue boxes marked, "CHRISTMAS DECORATIONS."

Just then we heard someone knocking at the front door. We ran for the door and threw it open, only to find Dad with the best Christmas tree we had ever seen.

We helped Dad bring it into the living room, but decided that our treats would come first before any more work. You know it takes lots of energy for a guy to find treasures.

We planned to do the decorations first and then, this afternoon, we can build a snowman. Grandpa has the perfect hat and cane we can borrow.

MISTLETOE MADNESS

I almost forgot. The Marshall Family wishes you a Happy Holiday Season and May All Your Dreams Come True in the New Year!

Barbara Hollace

MISTLETOE MADNESS

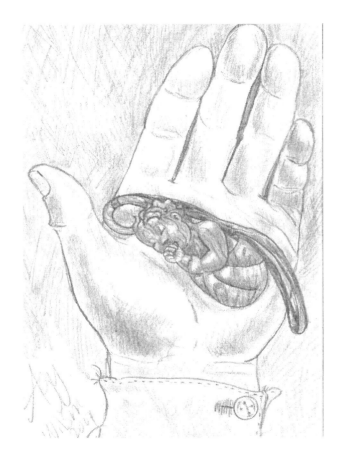

Illustration by Agy Wilson

Carving Out A Christmas

Dad calls himself a visionary.
Mom called him a dreamer.
I am not sure what I call him.

When Dad can't pick up a job at one of the chemical plants, he heads for the bay to fish. He takes chunks of wood and carves them 'to find out what's inside.' He brings home hummingbirds with headphones, zebras with earrings, ostriches with skateboards, sharks with umbrellas, and other zany creations. During these times, we eat lots of fish.

The one job we can count on is Dad working the Galveston Holiday Market. The four weekends following

207

MISTLETOE MADNESS

Thanksgiving have everyone in the county shopping for holiday arts and crafts. Dad always has a space in the back, at the end of the shell road. He sells trees— Christmas trees.

Before the Market officially opens, Dad picks out the best tree for us. He then loads it with his carved 'masterpieces' to sell. For all my fourteen years, I've heard, "Chip, one day people will wake up and appreciate this fine art of woodcarving. Orders will tumble in, and we'll celebrate with a fine mess of gumbo."

Dad dreams of being a fulltime craftsman with his own shop. He longs to do what he was 'put on this good earth to do.' He says he will carve us a two-story house, when he gets a tree that big.

Dad also enjoys people. He loves telling stories to the neighborhood kids using his carvings as characters. Everyone asks him for more stories. He says it is all part of his vision.

Until now, I believed him.

Mom was our glue,
but she got sick,
and we started to come undone.

208

MISTLETOE MADNESS

Last spring, after one of her treatments, Mom was arranging photos in an album when she sat up and chuckled. "Just look at this dad of yours and all his toys. He is such a boy. Your dad—the toy maker and dreamer extraordinaire." She held up a picture for me to see.

I got up from reading my comic book to see Dad looking like Noah among his animals.

Mom took a deep breath. "You know, Chip, you and I are a big part of his dream. I guess your dad wasn't counting on me getting so sick. I've tried to be there, helping with financial decisions, but he's so darn giving. He's always looking out for the little guy. He's a good man, and won't compromise what he believes. The only thing sharper than that blade of his is his faith. He loves us with his whole heart, but he loves God with his whole being."

Mom stopped smiling. "Son, promise me you'll look out for him and see he makes his way. Remember, you two are more than a team; you're my family, and . . ." Mom became quiet. She bit her lip and looked away.

I hugged her. "Mom, don't worry, I'll look after him. I promise."

209

MISTLETOE MADNESS

She held on to me, nodding.
That's when I knew; I would have to be the glue.

That same afternoon,
Mom told me a story
about us.

"You know," she began, "One of our best Christmases ever was when you were just two years old." Mom caught her breath. "Oh, it's funny now, but at the time, I was so angry. It was a cold, drizzly morning, so your dad and I kept warm by hammering pieces of wood together for tree stands. This couple with a toddler came up to me. The man asked if we had any ten-dollar trees. I blurted, 'You want a Christmas tree for ten bucks?' The man nodded with a shrug. Your father spun around and said, 'Sorry, sir, we just ran out. You should have been here sooner.' The woman smiled, picked up the boy and started to walk off. Your father didn't miss a beat, 'But we do have this one.' He pointed to *our* Noble Fir. 'We're finished using it as a display.' The man and woman looked at the tree, then at each other. Your dad stayed so serious, 'I'll still have to charge you five dollars for it.'

MISTLETOE MADNESS

The couple got so excited; they couldn't believe it. Neither could I. Your dad quickly plucked off his ornaments and took their five dollars. The family left beaming, but I was steaming. I growled at your dad, 'You're a pretty clever businessman, giving away a little of our Christmas to strangers.' He turned to me and said, 'Christmas isn't about business.' Then he winked and went on to the next customer. By nightfall, I had to admit he had done the right thing. Your dad isn't the Wall Street type, but he does know value. We still laugh about him selling a *used* Christmas tree."

I grinned and nodded along, since it sounded just like Dad.

Mom continued, "Oh, that night was rich. It was just you, your dad, and me. We feasted on chicken 'n dumplings and each had a present under a squatty, lopsided, balding tree. It was the best Christmas ever." Mom squeezed my hand. "So, son keep an eye on him for me."

I squeezed her hand back.

Mom went on arranging pictures. She never again talked about Dad and me being without her. She died two weeks later. She didn't get to finish the album. But, no

211

MISTLETOE MADNESS

matter—Dad won't look at it anyway.

Mom's big brother
had been her only hero,
until Dad came along

For three weeks, it's been Dad and me selling trees along that shell road in the back of the Market. Dad's fished a lot since Mom's passing in May, so we have a slew of ornaments. He's even entered one of them, a carved White Buffalo, for the Market's Arts and Crafts Contest. He enters something different every year. He never wins.

Mrs. Peterson always wins first place. One year she won first and second. Dad says she figures out who the judges are and then makes crafts to their interests. But knowing that and losing doesn't seem to bother Dad. He seems more disturbed that people don't appreciate woodcarvings. He thinks graffiti and plastic are people's preference for art.

When I was born, Dad took an old canopy frame from Mom's childhood bed and carved an infant Jesus. The Savior looks like me and is sucking his thumb like I did. Mom would cry every Christmas as she pulled it out of the shoebox. She'd say it was Dad, Jesus, and me, all wrapped up in one exquisite carving. I think it's neat, and it's mine. Dad calls it my keepsake. He went on to sculpt the whole nativity set from the remaining pieces of the canopy frame. Joseph looks like him, Mary looks like Mom, and some of the barn animals resemble our relatives.

This year, when Dad and I set up the booth, Dad handed me the shoebox, and pointed with his chin toward our tree of ornaments. I knew it was up to me to place each figurine, just the way Mom had, under the tree. I walked over and stooped down to begin. That's when I recognized Uncle Jack's booming voice calling out to Dad.

"Gonna sell lots of trees?"

"You bet," Dad answered.

"Yeah, well I hope it's enough to pay off what you owe. We really need the dough."

When Mom got sick, it was Uncle Jack who loaned Dad the money to pay the doctors for the operation.

"Sure, Jack. I'm thankful you helped us when we

were hurting."

"Yeah . . . you act like you ain't hurting now."

Dad didn't answer.

"I don't know your plans about staying around or heading out, but how do you expect to raise that boy of yours?"

Dad frowned. "You been drinking, Jack?"

Uncle Jack clinched his fists to his side and took a step towards Dad. "What's it to you?"

Dad looked down, without moving back.

Uncle Jack talked louder, "My sister falls in love with a whittler and dies a poor woman, and now her son's skipping school to care for his dad. What kind of man are you? You don't understand anything about providing for a family. I don't know how you can . . ."

Uncle Jack turned sideways and saw me kneeling at the tree.

I looked at Dad and swallowed hard.

Uncle Jack kicked and sprayed shells from the road into the field. He turned back to face Dad. "Sorry, man. I know you're doing your best. It's just . . . nothing seems right anymore."

Dad turned away.

214

MISTLETOE MADNESS

Uncle Jack shook his head. "Sorry, Chip," he muttered and walked past me to leave.

With one hand Dad covered his eyes and walked out toward the bay. He was praying.

Deep within me, a flame ignited. I just knelt there, not knowing who I was mad at most—Uncle Jack, Dad, or God.

That evening, when Dad came back, he told me how much we owed. I was good at budgeting, but there was no way to pay the bills *and* Uncle Jack, even if we sold all the trees.

I tried to think of other ways to earn money, but Dad told me he was "all tuckered out" and went on to bed.

All I wanted to do was run and get away from this place until no one around knew who I was—a dreamer's son raising a dad.

Have you ever broken something
that can't be fixed with glue,
or tape, or tears?

This morning, the last day of the Market, I blew up at Dad. By the look on his face, I know I hurt him. I didn't realize I had such a short fuse. It happened so fast.

A tall man in a suit came up to Dad and asked, "Who is the artisan of these fine carvings?"

Dad smiled and said, "I did these ornaments, and they're all for sale."

"I'm not talking about ornaments." The man reached down and picked up Mary. "It's this Nativity set that I want to know more about. Did you do the work?"

"Yes sir," Dad said.

"How much you asking for it?"

Dad began to sway, a sign he was nervous. "Well, it's really not for sale."

"Oh come on, everything has a price." The man reached into his coat pocket. "I'll make it worth your while." He brought out a thick money clip. "You'll have a nice Christmas with this wad."

Dad sighed. He shuffled his feet. He stared at the man's money.

"Would you take two hundred dollars?"

Dad's head shot back. I'm sure in disbelief.

The man grinned, "Okay then, how about two hundred fifty?"

Dad found his voice, "Well sir, I can sell you the

set, but this Jesus ain't for sale."

"What? That's the whole point of the Nativity."

Dad was strong. "I can make you another one, and send it to you later."

"Make the other one for yourself. I've got a plane to catch. This is a gift for my boss. How can I tell him Jesus doesn't come with the Nativity until next year? You people don't make sense."

Dad frowned and placed Mary back under the tree. "Sorry, no deal."

"Okay, okay then . . . four hundred dollars, including Jesus?"

Dad shook his head.

The man grunted, stuffed the money in his pocket, and left.

Dad went on to help a lady load a tree into her car. I stood stunned.

What was the matter with Dad? I made my way from the cash box to our tree and picked up Jesus. Where else could we get such money? It was a great business deal, and Dad just let it walk away!

That flickering flame fanned into a fire, and it started searing my senses.

MISTLETOE MADNESS

I ran up to him and yelled, "What did you do that for? Why didn't you ask me? Aren't I supposed to be your partner?"

Dad's mouth opened, but no words came out.

"Uncle Jack is right. You don't understand anything about business. You're nothing but a dreamer." I held the figurine close to his face. "This Jesus is mine, and I'm gonna sell him."

Dad tried to say something, but I shoved Jesus into my pocket and hurried to find the man.

I searched everywhere, but no one had seen a man in a suit. The whole time I looked, I felt miserable and mad – at Mom's dying and Dad's dreaming. Nothing was right. Why couldn't Dad be strong—like Mom? Why couldn't I?

I had to devise a plan. I figured I'd go live with Uncle Jack for awhile and get a job. It sounded logical and reasonable, but my mind kept replaying Dad's face flinching from my fury, and then my promise to Mom that I'd look out for Dad. I felt I might split in two, like a tree bursting from a lightning hit.

One last time, I scanned the grounds; the man was nowhere. When I turned toward the bay, something snapped and then crumbled inside me. I stopped, sat on a stump, and burning tears began to fall. I couldn't help it; I had given up.

For a long while, I sat there numb. My scorched mind had finally become cold and quiet. Hollowness had settled in. If I were a chunk of wood for one of Dad's carvings, he'd find nothing inside.

Finally, I stood up and took a deep breath. I pulled out my keepsake and stared at him. "Well Jesus, now what do I do?"

I can't say He answered me, but I did get an idea—a crazy, dreamer's idea.

Glue, tape, and tears

I stayed away all afternoon, not ready to go back and face Dad. When I did return, he wasn't at our tree lot. I went to check the cash box. On its shelf was Mom's photo album—opened. Dad had broken, too. Now I had to find him.

"Ladies and Gentlemen . . ." I could hear the emcee getting ready to officially close the Market. That's where Dad must be. I made it to the crowd surrounding the stage. I crawled on top of a barrel to look for him.

Dad was standing near the judges' stand.

"And now for fourth place—Mrs. Sanchez for her decorated Nutcracker." It was the announcement of the winners of the Arts and Crafts Contest.

"And third place goes to—Mr. Williams for his carved White Buffalo."

It was Dad. The man had called out Dad's name— He'd won!

Dad looked like he was in slow motion receiving his prize envelope.

I tried to wave, but he couldn't see me. I yelled, "Dad, hey Dad!"

He searched the crowd to find me. Finally, our eyes met, and I cupped my hands together and shook them above my head to show him congratulations.

"Second place—Mrs. Peterson, for her Bay Leaf Wreath and Garlic Garland."

Mrs. Peterson was already halfway up the steps. She graciously accepted the envelope without looking into it.

Dad, on the other hand, was waving his two one hundred dollar bills around for everyone to see.

MISTLETOE MADNESS

"And now for first place, who will receive seven hundred dollars and represent us at State, it's—Mr. Williams, again."

I froze.

Dad looked around confused.

". . . winning this time, for this carved Baby Jesus."

Dad looked at the announcer, then to Jesus, and then to me.

"And Ladies and Gentlemen, Jesus is sucking his thumb!"

Everyone laughed and started to applaud.

I don't remember getting over to Dad. I just knew I was hugging him and telling him, "Dad, a dream's come true, a dream's come true."

We were both laughing and crying when the emcee put the microphone to Dad's face. "Mr. Williams, excuse me, but many people want to know how much you're asking for the carving?"

Dad looked to me.

I took the microphone and said, "Folks, we'll be glad to take orders, but THIS JESUS AIN'T FOR SALE."

Charles Trevino

Joy of Christmas

The sleigh bells ring and jingle,
And Santa's coming soon!

Children all are laughing,
Parents say "I love you."
People keep on talking,
About alot of things.

Family comes to visit
With presents all for me!
Everythings so beautiful
As far as eye can see.

Snow just keeps on falling,
And stars are twinkling.

MISTLETOE MADNESS

The wind whispers secrets
To the snow covered pines,
Things are just so beautiful
At Christmas time.

Lucia de León

Mrs. Whipple's Christmas

Mrs. Whipple was my next-door neighbor growing up. Actually, since we lived in a pretty busy apartment complex, I had lots of neighbors. But Mrs. Whipple's living room window was right across from my bedroom window, and so I'd say that she definitely lived "next door."

Mrs. Whipple's husband, Mr. Whipple, had died just after Thanksgiving, and as Christmas approached I watched the rest of the street light up with candles in the windows and blinking lights around the eaves. But not Mrs. Whipple. She sat on her couch each day, staring at an empty TV set.

How did I know it wasn't on? Simple: Usually, I

could see the action reflecting off of her big, thick glasses. But for the past week there had been nothing. I didn't think she'd even turned her TV on since her husband passed away. There, in the corner of the living room, sat the coat rack. His hat and coat still hung there, as if perhaps he might come home one day and surprise Mrs. Whipple and ask, "Darling, why haven't you turned on the TV in three whole weeks?"

Christmas at our house was always a pretty big deal, and come the big day, I didn't have much time to think about poor, old Mrs. Whipple. There were presents to open in the morning and then, in the afternoon, candles to light and the front door to answer and big, heavy, winter coats to take from the likes of Uncle Mort and Cousin Shirley. There were pickles to steal off the relish tray, model planes to hide from my older nephew Chuck, and kisses to avoid from Granny Hermanek.

"Answer that, Benjy," said my Mom, amid all the hustle and bustle, as yet another guest arrived. This time it was Aunt Bernice, famous for her double-chocolate candy cane pies. That Christmas, however, she had brought something new: A smoked turkey!

"It's imported," she bragged. "All the way from

MISTLETOE MADNESS

Wisconsin. You didn't cook one of your own, did you dear?"

My mom shook her head, although I knew she'd been basting a twenty-pound bird for the last six hours. "Quick," she said to me, pulling hers out of the oven and handing me two fat, itchy oven mitts. "Take this turkey to the front office. I'm sure the girls up there are still working, and they could enjoy a little treat. Hurry, before Bernice sees you!"

And so, out into the chilly afternoon I went, lugging a twenty-pound turkey on my little red wagon and trying to avoid roving dogs and swooping crows. Up and down the sidewalk I went, until finally I arrived at our apartment complex's front office. Inside I could hear Christmas carols, and the girls who Mom thought would be so lonely and hungry were taking advantage of the slow business day by munching on gingerbread and dancing to the radio.

I thought about going in, but figured they didn't need the turkey half as much as someone else I knew. And so back up and down the sidewalk I went, until I stood at the door of old Mrs. Whipple, still bore the sad, black wreath that had been up since just after Thanksgiving.

MISTLETOE MADNESS

I knocked on the door, and was tempted to simply run away, leaving the donated turkey behind, but old Mrs. Whipple wasn't as slow as I thought. Zing! went the door as it opened after only two knocks. Had she been waiting just on the other side for a chance guest? I wondered silently.

"I-I-I brought you a turkey," I managed to stutter. "Merry Christmas!"

Tears filled old Mrs. Whipple's eyes as she looked up at the heavens. "You finally sent someone who cares," was all she managed to say before swooping me up and inviting me inside with her.

There, I had the quickest Christmas dinner of my life. Old Mrs. Whipple whooped and hollered and, since she hadn't been expecting visitors, complained that there was no dessert.

Finding her coat, I invited her back to our house. "We've got six desserts," I bragged.

Mrs. Whipple tasted each and every one.

Rusty Fischer

MISTLETOE MADNESS

Illustration by Elsbet Vance

228

Liranel's Gift

Liranel perched on her cushioned window seat above the courtyard and rubbed her aching feet. They always hurt worse in the winter. She shivered and wrapped herself more tightly in her woolen cloak. Despite the cheery fire in the hearth and the thick tapestries on the walls, it was cold in the castle.

Her friend Paul, the fourteen-year-old kitchen boy, was carefully crossing the courtyard's icy cobblestones, a bucket swinging from either hand. Liranel waved at him through the thick glass. He grinned impudently up at her and disappeared through the door just below her window. She'd missed him this morning; usually he accompanied her and Nan up the steep trail to Old Cate's, but today he'd been needed to help in the kitchen.

Nan bustled into Liranel's room, bringing a draft of the chilly air from the corridor with her.

"Here, now, let me do that," she said, catching Liranel in the act of rubbing her feet again.

She pulled a stool closer, and propped one twisted foot and then the other in her lap. Liranel groaned as her nursemaid massaged and prodded the tight muscles. Her feet always felt better after Nan had finished, but during, it was akin to torture.

A chirurgeon had broken the bones of Liranel's turned-in feet and ankles when she had been six months old, insisting that it was the only way a child born with clubfeet could ever walk straight. The Duke had bowed to superior medical knowledge then, but had later banished the man from his lands. The broken bones had healed oddly, and Liranel's feet were misshapen lumps. The discovery that gentle manipulation would have worked better had come far too late.

"How's this?" asked Nan, probing at a particularly tender spot. She nodded in satisfaction as Liranel yelped. "I do wish you'd ride your pony."

"Oh, Nan," said Liranel, "but then I would have to

ask the stablemaster, and he would have to get Father's permission, and then I would have to explain why I wanted Jewel . . ." Easier to walk, by far. Talking to her father, Duke Trieste, was difficult at the best of times.

"But at least, then, I might be able to ride, too," said Nan.

"I'm sorry, Nan," said Liranel.

"Na, na, child, I shouldn't complain. If you can make it, then surely I can," said Nan. "I don't know how you do it, truly I don't."

Liranel had been on crutches ever since she'd been taught to walk. By now, she was quite handy with them, but the trail to Old Cate's was long, and these days, slippery with packed snow. She'd had to be extra careful, and that had made her muscles tense.

"I had to go, Nan. I promised Cate I'd visit her today," said Liranel. "She's lonely, since she has no children of her own. Besides, she liked my gift."

Old Cate had chuckled when she'd opened the fabric wrapper and discovered the carved wooden sheep nestled within. It had looked just like one of hers.

"A lovely Twelfth Night gift," Nan agreed. "I would have enjoyed the walk more, had I not had to carry that basket."

Liranel hid a smile. Nan grumbled, but never seemed to mind the chance to put her feet up for an hour or so when they finally got to Old Cate's snug cave. Nan dozed in front of the smoky fire while Liranel listened to the old woman recount the ancient tales, the hum of her spinning wheel increasing or decreasing according to the rhythm of her voice.

Liranel tried to visit Old Cate at least once a month at her cave high in the hills behind the castle. Liranel swung along on her crutches while Nan huffed and puffed behind, carrying whatever they had been able to scrounge from the kitchens. They'd already gone once this month, just before Christmas, so today's offering had been an extra donation. Cate had certainly seemed grateful for it. Winters were hard on the old woman.

They were hard on Liranel's feet and legs, too. Yet Nan's hands were firm but gentle, and already Liranel's muscles were feeling less like iron rods and more like human flesh. Nan dug her thumbs into a tight knot high up near Liranel's left knee and Liranel groaned.

"Oh, yes, right there," she said.

Nan sighed. "Giving charity was something your

mother did too."

"I don't remember much about my mother," said Liranel, almost to herself. She only had a few foggy images of a kind-faced blonde woman dressed in blue. Duchess Mariana had died when Liranel had been just two, crushed in an avalanche while returning home from a Singing. "I think I remember her Singing me lullabies, though."

"Sh, now, no mention of Singing," Nan admonished. "You know how your father feels about that."

Yes. Liranel's mother had been a Singer. Not just a singer, a *Singer*. Singing and Songs were more than just music; they helped to keep the world in balance. No birth, death, marriage, or other celebration was complete without Singing, for the magic of the Songs evoked the spirits that resided in everything: the people, the animals, the plants and rocks—even the very air itself—and kept them in harmony.

In some places, Liranel had heard, they even greeted the sun each morning with Songs.

Not here, in Castle Trieste, however. Music wasn't forbidden, but no one was allowed to Sing. The simple tunes of the peasants were all right, and the Duke did allow hymns in chapel and church. Liranel loved listening to both, especially the hymns. But Singers and Songs were not permitted. Liranel had never been brave enough to ask anyone why her father hated Singers and their Songs so much. Perhaps he had hated her mother, for bringing such a disabled child into the world.

The problem was, only eleven days ago, at dawn on her twelfth birthday, Liranel had discovered that she was a Singer, too. She'd been happy, she remembered, looking out her window at the beautiful morning, and the Song had just burst from her lips. She had no idea where it came from; it was just there. It was only good fortune that no one but Paul had been around to hear it. He'd been delighted, but had promised to keep her secret. Ever since, Liranel had worried that she might accidentally Sing sometime when her father was nearby. Then he would know, and she would be banished.

That was the worst part—she would have to leave Castle Trieste. The thought saddened her. Even if the stone castle was old and drafty, and cold in winters, she loved it. This was her home!

Liranel worried about how she would survive on

her own, trying to get about on her mangled feet. The streets of the town below the castle were smooth and gently sloped, but other places wouldn't be. Perhaps she would be allowed to take her pony, Jewel. Well, she would just have to make her way somehow. It would be nice if she could take Nan, too, but was it fair to take her faithful nurse with her on what might be a dangerous journey?

She swallowed. "You're so good to me, Nan."

"And so I am," said Nan, "and so I should be. You are a good child, Liranel. Old Cate knows it."

"I'm glad we were able to take her so much today," said Liranel, remembering the full basket. "Cook was generous."

Nan snorted. "Cook? It was your little friend Paul who packed the basket this time, without Cook's knowledge. Just as well, too. It's a feast day, and Cook is in a terrible tizzy."

"What is it this time?" asked Liranel.

Cook had a real name, but no one ever used it. He was always in a "tizzy" over something. Liranel had never met a fussier fellow, ever up in arms about this or that. He was a wonderful chef, though.

MISTLETOE MADNESS

"It seems someone left the eels out overnight in the courtyard and the water in their tubs froze solid," said Nan, chuckling. "He doesn't know what they'll taste like once they've thawed. And you can be assured that once he finds out who was responsible, life won't be worth living for that individual."

"How can they taste any worse than they already do?" asked Liranel, wrinkling her nose.

"Eels are good for you," Nan admonished. "They strengthen your liver. There."

She set Liranel's feet back on the cushioned seat and gently eased them into the thick felt slippers that Liranel wore inside the castle. Never would she be able to wear anything like a lady's dainty footwear.

Liranel looked out the window. It was snowing again, big fat flakes that drifted silently to the ground out of a leaden sky. It had been a lovely clear blue this morning, when she and Nan had made the trip up the rocky path to Old Cate's with the basket of food.

"So what other masterpieces does Cook have in mind for the feast?" asked Liranel. Tonight's meal would be even more elaborate than the one they'd had on the first day of Christmas. That had been a solemn, quiet day, but on the twelfth and final day, there would be entertainment and gifts and merriment.

"You've enough curiosity to choke a cat, haven't you? You know Cook," said Nan. "He won't say. He likes his little secrets, he does. Now don't you go trying to pry it out of him. Mind you, I did spot a large bowl of dried rose petals on one of the kitchen tables."

"Oh! Rose pudding?" asked Liranel. It was one of her favorites.

"Possibly, possibly," said Nan, nodding. "Or it may be for a subtlety."

Liranel nodded. Cook liked to surprise Duke Trieste with his culinary concoctions, and incredible food sculptures called subtleties. Liranel wasn't sure why they were called that since they were always spectacular; none of them were in the least bit "subtle." Sometimes they weren't even edible!

"Well, eels and rose petals aside, you should be getting ready," said Nan.

Liranel brightened. The feast would take her mind off her problems.

"Yes!" she said. "Which should I wear, Nan, the red dress or the green one?"

MISTLETOE MADNESS

Nan pursed her lips. "I suppose either of them would be suitable for the season," she said, rising. She skirted Liranel's canopied bed and reached for the handle of her wooden wardrobe. "But I think I might have something even better."

Triumphantly, she swung the door wide. Liranel gasped. Royal blue velvet spilled out, revealing a gown with a long train and a bodice cut low like a lady's. Cloth-of-gold sleeves completed the dress. It was lengthy enough to cover her unsightly felt slippers, too.

"Oh, Nan!" said Liranel.

Nan smiled. "I've had the seamstresses sewing day and night for a week. After all, you will be the Lady of the Feast tonight, as is your right and your duty."

"I'm to be at the High Table?" Liranel squeaked.

"Of course. You're of age now. Had you forgotten?" Nan teased.

"Oh," Liranel said faintly. Her birthday was on St. Stephen's Day, right after Christmas. "Almost a Christmas baby," Nan was fond of saying. Liranel's discovery of her disastrous talent had scrambled her wits and forced the memory of this honor from her mind. It meant that she'd be sitting in far too close proximity to her father. Her fists clenched. What if she couldn't control herself? Liranel's excitement about the feast drained away.

"It will be good to see someone at the High Table with your father again," said Nan. "It was your mother's place. Ah, well. Your father will meet you outside the Hall. Have you given him his gift yet?"

"No, I was going to give it to him at the feast," said Liranel. She pointed to her bed, where the little carved wooden box with its inlaid glass lid lay. "Paul helped me pick it out when we went to the market. I thought Father might use it for his pens."

"It's very pretty," said Nan. "Don't forget it, now."

The sky was darkening. Nan rose and set about lighting the tapers and thick tallow candles that graced Liranel's bedroom.

Behind her back, Liranel rolled her eyes. Nan still treated her like a child sometimes.

Liranel balanced on her twisted feet and reached into the wardrobe, pulling the dress off its hanger. The velvet was lovely and plush and the cloth-of-gold crinkled softly in her hands.

Ever since last year, it had been a point of pride

for Liranel to be able to dress herself. Sometimes she wished she hadn't made her demand so noisily clear. It would be too humiliating to ask for help now. At least this outfit's outer dress had lacing up the sides to pull it tight, which was something she could do for herself.

She did allow Nan to dress her hair, looping strings of the pearls that Duke Trieste's sea-holdings were so famous for through Liranel's dark russet locks. She admired the effect in the tiny mirror at her vanity table, then inspected her face. She was pale from lack of sleep, but then she was always pale. Nan often praised her milk-white skin. No blemishes, anyway. Liranel hoped no one would notice the slight grayness under her blue eyes.

Liranel tucked her father's gift inside her belt pouch and she and Nan made their way down the corridor to the Great Hall. It was just as well Liranel's bedroom was on the same floor. She wasn't sure she could manage stairs in the new long skirt.

Liranel waited alone in the entranceway, sitting on a bench rather than standing, for her father. She had propped her crutches against the wall, half-hidden behind a tapestry embroidered with a hunt scene. Nan was already in the Hall, seated at one of the higher tables, and

Paul, of course, would be in the kitchen.

The Duke, a tall man, came striding around a corner, speaking earnestly with one of his knights. It was Sir Thomas who saw Liranel first, his face breaking into a wide grin.

"My Lady!" said Sir Thomas, taking her hand and lightly brushing a kiss across her knuckles. "You are the very image of your lovely mother, blessed be her soul."

"Am I?" said Liranel. She dimpled, feeling a flush rising from her neck.

She glanced at her father. He looked as though he were about to say something, but then his eyes darkened and he looked away. Liranel wished that Sir Thomas hadn't mentioned her mother, but he seemed oblivious to his mistake.

"Come," said the Duke.

He and Sir Thomas waited while Liranel retrieved her crutches from behind the wall hanging. They courteously kept their pace as slow as her own halting gait. Beyond that first word, the Duke said nothing more.

Sir Thomas pushed the wide wooden door open. The Duke's Herald pounded a hollow wooden box mounted on the floor with the end of his staff to make it echo, and announced them.

"His Grace, the Duke of Trieste, his daughter, the Lady Liranel, and Sir Thomas Riley," he said, in round, ringing tones that Liranel admired. The Herald was a man who knew how to be heard across the babble of a hundred voices.

The assembled nobles and guests clapped as the three of them entered. Some faltered as Liranel stumped her way into the hall, but renewed the applause when they realized their error. The applause continued until they were all seated at the High Table. Sir Thomas seated Liranel in the high-backed chair next to her father, patted her shoulder, and sat on her other side.

"Is your lady wife not attending tonight?" Liranel asked politely, seeing that he was sharing his plate with no one. As was customary at feasts, couples shared one plate. She would be sharing hers with her father.

Sir Thomas grimaced. "She's at home, my lady. Our little boy was born only a week ago, and she is not yet well enough to travel."

"Was she troubled by it?" Liranel sipped from her silver wine cup, and made a face. The wine, which she usually drank well-watered, was stronger than she expected.

"No," said Sir Thomas, smiling. Liranel wasn't sure if he was smiling at the thought of his son, or at her face. "It's just that it's a long way to come, even for such a feast as this." He sighed then. "I only wish . . ." He stopped, his gaze on the Duke, who was absently munching nutmeats from a bowl placed in front of him.

"Yes?" said Liranel.

Sir Thomas shook his head, and dug into his own nut bowl. "Nothing."

But Liranel knew what he had been about to say. The birth needed a Singing. The babe might yet sicken and die because of it, his little spirit not yet in harmony with its surroundings. Duke Trieste's lands were doing well enough, but there had been problems: crops failing for no good reason; herds of sheep getting more than their fair share of illnesses. Even the animals of the forest were becoming scarce. Only Old Cate's little herd of sheep seemed to do well. She claimed it was the clean mountain air that kept them healthy.

Liranel almost blurted out to Sir Thomas that she could help. Perhaps if she sneaked out to his home, somehow . . . but wouldn't he be honor-bound to tell the

MISTLETOE MADNESS

Duke about it then? The suggestion died on Liranel's lips, and she closed them firmly.

"Oh, look," said Sir Thomas, drawing her attention to the door from the kitchens. Cook preened as he preceded two men carrying a towering confection of bread dough on a trestle between them. The bread had been baked in the shape of the Duke's personal crest, a bear rising on its hind legs to paw at the air. Its nose and claws had been painted gold.

Liranel had no idea how Cook had made the bear look so real, and judging by the roar of the crowd, neither had anyone else. The Duke applauded enthusiastically and threw Cook a coin. Cook bowed to the High Table and retreated to the kitchen, obviously well-pleased with himself.

The subtlety signaled the first course. There were the detested eels, but Cook had provided other dishes as well, including a mushroom pasty and a stew of chicken in rosewater.

"Do you know what's first for the entertainment?" Sir Thomas asked over Liranel's head.

"Acrobats," grunted the Duke.

As soon as the dishes had all been served, several

gaily dressed boys and girls tumbled into the open space in front of the High Table, leaping and whooping, some of them standing on each other's shoulders, still more twisting themselves into impossible shapes.

"Hhuuu-up!" said a tiny blonde girl with bells on her toes, who could not have been more than four years old. She cartwheeled down the long stretch of tables, posed in front of the High Table, then cartwheeled back up the other side. Everyone laughed. The acrobats finished to a round of applause.

The dishes were removed and more served, and while they ate the second course, a troupe of mummers acted out the story of Saint Simeon, who had waited all his life for the Savior to appear and was finally given the gift of seeing him just before he died.

The third course was apparently going to be preceded by yet another of Cook's masterpieces. The noise from the crowd of feast-goers slowly settled into silence as a large, exotically painted wooden crate was trundled into the room on squeaky rollers. Liranel peered at it. She thought she could hear snuffling noises emanating from the box.

Paul, who had been helping to pull the ropes

attached to the crate, scrambled up the side and tugged at the latch on the top of the box. At once, all the sides of the box fell outward and slammed to the floor with a series of cracks. Many in the crowd screamed as they saw what the box held.

A bear! A live bear! Safely caged, to be sure, with iron bars all around, but even so! Its long curved claws were gilded with gold paint, just like the Duke's crest. There wasn't much room in the cage, and the bear sat huddled in a corner, its back pressed up against the bars. Cook was trying to get it to stand, raising his arms and shouting commands. The bear ignored him. Several people laughed.

"Oh, the poor thing," said Liranel.

"Who?" said Sir Thomas, who was grinning at Cook's antics. "Him, or the beast?"

"The bear," said Liranel. "It's winter. It should be asleep, shouldn't it?" The bear looked cranky.

"I suppose," said Sir Thomas.

The tiny girl acrobat, fascinated by the bear, was edging closer to its cage. She stroked the animal's black fur through the bars, then daringly poked it.

Startled, the bear let out a growl and stood

abruptly. The cage fell over, and the lid popped off with a clang. Instantly, the bear was out, its huge paws sweeping the air.

It connected with Cook, who skidded down the floor, four parallel scratches in the back of his tunic oozing blood. He lay still where he stopped. The bear, roaring, finally stood on its hind legs, its front paws high in the air, mirroring the crest on the wall behind the Duke.

The little girl acrobat screeched as the bear's gaze fastened on her. Its front paws landed on the floor with a reverberating double thump. The bear paced toward the little girl, its wedge-shaped head swinging from side to side. The girl scrambled under one of the tables and the feast-goers there screamed as the bear approached them.

Liranel's father stood and fumbled for his sword, but, of course, he had not worn it to the feast. The best he had was the knife with which he had cut their meat. Yelling, he brandished the knife, and leapt over the High Table to confront the animal, trying to draw the bear's attention.

The bear took one look at this new threat and its lips rippled back, showing the sharp, yellowed fangs. It paced toward Liranel's father. The Duke waited with his knife held out in front of him. Its blade was pitifully small when compared to the bear's claws and teeth.

An archer on the upper balcony drew his bow, but hesitated, unable to get a clear shot around the Duke. The feast-goers were frozen in their places, all except for Paul, who was creeping around behind the animal, but what could he possibly do?

The bear rose on its hind legs again, pawing the air and roaring. The Duke took a step back, then swallowed and stepped forward once more, making stabbing motions at the bear.

"Father!" Liranel screamed. She stood, bracing herself against the table. There was no way he could survive this! Perhaps if she could distract the animal—but with what? Liranel reached into her pouch and drew out the little carved box. As her father prepared to attack, she threw it. It arced upwards, flashing in the light from the torches. The bear ducked, but kept advancing, and the box crashed to the floor.

The bear lunged for the Duke. Something else? No. There wasn't time, now. There was only one other way.

Liranel took a deep breath—and Sang. The Song

welled up from somewhere deep within her. It was a soothing Song, one that told the bear to be calm, that he was loved and appreciated, and that she knew he was tired and only wanted to go back to his snug cave in the forest.

The bear paused, seeming to listen. Then, slowly, it lowered to the ground, and ambled back to the remains of its cage where it lay down with a rumbling groan. Liranel's Song turned softer then, a crooning lullaby that sent the bear to sleep. It closed its eyes, then twitched once. The little girl acrobat giggled nervously when it began to snore.

As the last note of Liranel's Song trailed off, a sigh rippled around the Great Hall. Liranel let out a sigh of her own and collapsed, trembling, into her seat. Her feet ached.

Well, her secret was well and truly out now. Paul, next to a groggy Cook, grinned at her. She smiled faintly back. She glanced at Nan and almost laughed. Nan's mouth had dropped open.

Only then did Liranel dare to look at her father, the Duke. He was on his knees on the floor of the Great Hall, staring at his daughter as if he had never seen her before. Liranel steeled herself for his displeasure.

He stood and staggered a few steps forward, his face paling. "You, a Singer?" he whispered. "But how? You have no training . . ."

"I don't know how, Father," Liranel said wearily. The Song had tired her. "But it's what I was born to be."

For it was true. She *was* a Singer, forbidden or not. She knew that now. No one could alter that, not even her father.

In the silence, the Hall door creaked open and someone slipped inside, trailing snow. Liranel gave the latecomer a brief glance, but the person was so swathed in layers of clothing that she couldn't make out who it was.

"I'll go pack my things," said Liranel.

"What?" said her father.

"The banishment, Father. I must go."

"Liranel . . ." her father began.

Liranel hung her head. "I'm sorry, Father. I didn't mean to hurt you. As my mother did."

A great groan escaped from her father's throat, like the moan of a wounded animal. "Oh, daughter. How could you think that?"

Liranel frowned, puzzled. "Why else would you banish Singers?"

MISTLETOE MADNESS

Her father shook his head. "You don't understand. I loved your mother with all my soul. When she died, I banished them because I couldn't bear to hear Songs ever again. It was like a spear through my heart."

"And so you denied the Songs to all," said a new voice, a woman's voice. It was one that Liranel knew, but hadn't expected to hear, and it took her a moment to understand who it was. She turned to the door, where the latecomer was unwrapping the scarf that had hidden her face.

Liranel gasped. "Cate?"

Belying her years, the old woman strode forward into the hall. She walked behind the High Table, and laid an arm across Liranel's shoulders.

"Yes, dear one," she said, laughing. "I knew there was something different about you today, but I did not know what it was. Well done! I have been waiting for this day for a very long time."

Liranel stared at her. "What do you mean?"

"I was your mother's Singing teacher once," said Cate. "When she died, I came here, for I knew that someday you would need me."

"Do you tell me," demanded the Duke, "that I

have been sheltering a Singer all this time, unknown to me? Is that why my daughter Sang? Were you teaching her in secret?"

"No," said Cate, quite calmly. "I haven't been teaching Liranel anything more than the old tales. Which is something Singers do need to know, for it is they who pass them on to future generations. Or had you forgotten that?" She turned to Liranel. "But being a Singer—that Gift comes of itself, when it will."

Liranel nodded. Her so-called Gift had certainly showed up all by itself on her birthday, unwanted. "I know," she said softly.

Cate hugged Liranel, then turned to the Duke. "And you! Forbidding Singing on your lands! Your Grace, how could you deny that to your people?"

The Duke blinked in surprise at this bold, old woman. "It hurt so much," he whispered. "The memory."

"Tcha! Selfish man!" said Cate.

A smile touched Liranel's lips. She had never heard her old friend talk like this. And had certainly never heard anyone speak to the Duke so!

"I hadn't realized how much I missed the Singing," said Duke Trieste.

252

"Well, if you are sensible, you won't have to miss it any longer. You can't deny your daughter's Gift," said Cate. "Singers need to Sing."

"Singers go where they're needed," he protested. "Her mother was killed while journeying. What if she goes away from me, too?"

Cate chuckled. "On these mangled feet? No, there are others who can journey. Liranel can stay here at the castle, or with me, if need be, and those in need of Singing can come to her."

"I don't know enough yet," said Liranel.

"You did well with the bear," said Cate, "but yes, you still have much to learn."

"Would you teach me?" asked Liranel.

"I would be honored," said Cate.

Liranel retrieved her crutches and slowly made her way around the table. She gently touched her father's arm.

"Father?" she asked.

He looked at her and smiled tentatively. "I had thought your feet were a curse—but instead they are a blessing." He raised his head and his voice rang out across the room. "From this day forward, Singers are most welcome on my lands! We will have Songs again!"

MISTLETOE MADNESS

His people cheered. "All hail Duke Trieste! And his daughter, Lady Liranel the Singer!"

Liranel reached out her hand. The Duke clasped it tight in his own.

"Forgive me," he said. "In my grief, I lost sight of what truly matters."

"It's all right, Father," said Liranel. She glanced across the room at Paul, who had picked up the shattered bits of her little box and was vainly trying to piece them back together. "I wish I hadn't broken your gift," she said.

The Duke shook his head. "Liranel, you have given me something more precious than any trinket. You have given me back the gift of Song."

Liranel's heart lifted. The Gift of Song. Yes!

Leslie Carmichael

The Christmas Spirit

"Christmas vacation's here! Yeah!" Ten-year-old Jenny exclaimed as she walked into the candy store with Tim and José, her best friends since the first grade.

Jenny noticed Tim stood by the door while José and she looked at the treats on the display. *Tim is embarrassed again that Gram's small pension didn't allow for candy.* His parents died in a car accident when he was only a year old.

"My treat. You're both teaching me how to ski tomorrow," said Jenny giving José and Tim the bags filled with a rainbow of ribbon candy.

On the snowy sidewalk, José said. "Let's go to my house. Mom's baking her famous cookies."

MISTLETOE MADNESS

Jenny could almost smell the sweet aroma in the cold air. She glanced at Tim.

"Nah, I can't. I'm helping Gram again tonight." Tim pulled down the sleeves of his coat that he had outgrown last winter.

"Maybe later you can join my family," said Jenny, gently touching Tim's shoulder. She had a gift waiting for Tim under the Christmas tree.

"Thanks, but we're cleaning a big office on the other side of town. It's a huge job. Gram needs my help." Tim walked away. "I'll call you tonight. Thanks for the candy."

José and Jenny skipped down the street to their houses on opposite sides of the street.

"Wanna come and play a video game?" asked José.

"You think you can beat me this time?" Jenny smiled. Her eyes sparkled.

José's face turned red. "Maybe I will!" he yelled.

Red and white poinsettias in each corner brightened up the small foyer. The Christmas tree, up to the ceiling, took half the living room. There were boxes and boxes of gifts wrapped in funny-looking paper with pink roses. Jenny giggled.

"Mom ran out of the Christmas paper. But don't laugh. I'm getting The Track." José had begged his mom to get him this radio-controlled monster toy since his birthday last July. He opened the cookie jar. "Want one?"

Jenny nodded. "The Track, ha. Cool. I'll be over more often then." She winked grabbing the fresh-baked cookie. Soft and chewy, it melted in her mouth.

Knowing it would be the best present for her friend, Jenny let José win at the video game.

"I won! I won!" shouted José. He laughed and danced around the room.

Jenny giggled. *Boys are so funny,* she thought as she went home.

Jenny's Christmas tree, smaller than Jose's, had all her favorite ornaments. Jenny's family spent two evenings decorating the tree with the twinkling lights and the sparkling balls, the candy canes and the wooden toys, the popcorn garlands and the golden tinsel.

Jenny inhaled the fresh pine smell and twirled around the tree. "I love Christmas."

* * *

During dinner, the phone rang. Jenny rushed to

answer.

Tim's Gram cried on the other end. "Accident . . . Tim . . . Hospital . . ."

Jenny's face became pale. She held her breath for a moment as tears sprung to her eyes. She gasped for air as she whispered, "Accident . . . Tim . . ." *Maybe it didn't really happen. How could it? It's just a bad dream. When I wake up, Tim will be fine.*

But Tim's Gram still wept on the phone. "I can't lose Tim."

Jenny's father grabbed the phone from her weakening hand. "Yes, Mrs. Sosnowski. Please calm down. I can't understand a word you're saying. Okay . . . Okay . . . We'll be there. Soon . . . Very soon . . ."

Her heart knotted, Jenny rushed to the door without even taking her coat. With trembling fingers, she unlocked the latch and ran to the car. She shivered, but not from the cold wind.

On the way to the hospital, Jenny thought. *Poor Tim. He's going to spend Christmas in the hospital.* She turned to her father. "Tim's going to be okay, right?" Her heart stopped as she waited for the answer.

"Only the doctor can tell us."

MISTLETOE MADNESS

* * *

José was already at the hospital. He came running down the brightly lit corridor and took them to Tim's room. Tim's face was as white as the hospital walls; his eyes were closed. His left leg, in a cast, rested on a pillow. Many tubes went in and out of his body. Jenny held her breath and tried not to cry. But when she inhaled the hospital smells, she burst into tears.

José hugged her. "He'll get better. I know he will!"

They overheard the doctor say to Jenny's father, "Tim's leg is broken in three different places. He will require a series of surgeries. At this moment, we don't know if he will be able to walk again."

Jenny covered her sobs with her hands. *Oh, no. Tim's gram got him a new bike for Christmas.* She cried, "Poor Tim. He doesn't have a Christmas tree or a gift now." She knew what she had to do. *I hope the tree will fit into Tim's hospital room.*

She whispered to José, "Maybe Tim can play with The Track?"

But José shook his head. "No, I'm not giving him my track. You know, Jenny, how long it took me to

259

convince Mom to get it for me? No! Do you know how much it cost? No, no way." Still shaking his head, José walked away.

At least Tim will have a tree.

"Are you sure?" asked her father after she told him her plan in the car on the way back to the house.

Jenny nodded with a smile. "He can have it." *This is Christmas Eve, the night when miracles should happen.*

* * *

They made it back to the hospital after midnight. Jenny helped her father bring the Christmas tree up the hospital stairs. It filled the corridor with a fresh pine smell. The dangling ornaments created a soft melody as they carried the tree to Tim's room. The first thing they saw by his door was a big box wrapped in funny-looking paper with pink roses. "From Santa," said the note.

Eugina White

The Purple Christmas Ball with the Silver Tassel

Christmas was in full swing in the suburban city of Lexington, and Maxmall was teeming with shoppers looking for last-minute bargains.

Mrs. Ross was too busy looking for Christmas ornaments and paid no attention to the crowds. Men and security officers ran in all directions through the crowds, but Mrs. Ross kept to herself, concentrating on the Christmas ornaments that were marked down to less than half price.

Picking some pretty ornaments, Mrs. Ross was about to leave when her eyes fell on a huge purple

MISTLETOE MADNESS

Christmas ball with a silver tassel. The price was so reduced that she bought it on impulse. After checking out, she headed home.

Arriving at her house, she found the neighborhood in an upheaval. Her children and other kids ran to her car shouting: "The Christmas balls are being stolen!"

Excitedly, the kids talked all at once. Mrs. Ross, having had enough of loud crowds, calmly asked her two young ones to help her with the packages. Once inside she asked, "So, what happened?"

Her children said in one voice, "Robbed, Mom, robbed!" Mrs. Ross pleaded, "One at a time, please!"

The older one, Cindy, came forward, "The Christmas trees in the neighborhood have been robbed of their ornaments!"

Ricky, her youngest cut in, "No clues, Mom, not a trace!"

"That's strange," Mrs. Ross said, "who would steal Christmas ornaments? Maybe it's a joke or birds; birds like taking shiny things, you know."

Looking around Ricky said, "Birds? All the screens and doors are usually closed."

"Good thinking," said Mrs. Ross, "then it must be

someone playing a trick."

Offended, Cindy exclaimed, "That's mean! Playing a trick like that two days before Christmas! That's very mean!"

"At least our tree has no ornaments yet," said Mrs. Ross, "Father put the tree up for us to decorate. Let's hang the ornaments now so when Daddy comes he can add all the Christmas lights."

Mrs. Ross took off her street shoes and joined the children in the happy task of opening the boxes and hanging the balls. When Cindy came upon the purple ball with the silver tassel, she gasped, "Mother, it is so unusual, almost unreal!"

The purple ball looked very strange for a Christmas ornament. On both sides it had silver circles, and in the purple center of each circle was a solid, smaller circle of silver glitter. It resembled a big eye on a shiny purple field that seemed to look back at you from the bright purple ball. The thick, long silver tassel hanging under it was made of brilliant silver beads, making a striking, mystifying contrast.

Looking at the ball uneasily, Ricky said, "Yup, looks kind of weird to me."

MISTLETOE MADNESS

Moving the ball gently, Cindy said, "Mother, it rattles!"

Carefully, Mrs. Ross took the ball and said, "These balls are made of glass. Maybe some pieces of glass were left inside. Better to leave it alone."

She took a closer look and said, "Purple is not a Christmas color, but this purple is so bright! And the silver tassel is so becoming to the purple. Very unusual. Maybe that's why nobody bought it and it was so reduced. Anyway, I am glad I bought it."

Saying this, she hung the purple ball with the silver tassel right in the middle of the tree, so it faced everyone with its silvery gaze. Almost hypnotized, they looked up at it, the silver eye looking back at them.

Blinking her eyes, Mrs. Ross announced, "Well, we're finished. Let's wait for Daddy while I cook dinner." And she lost herself in the kitchen.

Cindy, fascinated by the purple ball said, "Hope it doesn't get stolen."

Ricky answered, "I will camp in front of the tree and won't let anyone touch it."

Cindy asked, "Can I camp with you? That ball looks like a flying saucer . . ."

MISTLETOE MADNESS

Puzzled, Ricky looked at her and said, "Cindy, you are talking silly. I will camp downstairs and watch that tree."

When Father arrived, they all had dinner and then he hung all the Christmas lights. Mother said happily, "Tomorrow night is Christmas Eve; at last we are ready for it!"

Cindy insisted, "Can I stay up and watch the tree with Ricky? Huh, Mom, huh, Daddy?"

After much arguing, it was decided that the children could camp downstairs for the night. Under his breath, Father told Mother as they went up the stairs, "Let them stay up, Amanda. After all it is their tree. This will give them a sense of responsibility. There must be a harmless explanation to these robberies. Don't worry, Mom, it is safe."

To stay awake, Cindy and Ricky told each other scary stories about flying saucers. They imagined saucers with laser beams that could suck Christmas ornaments right out of houses as they hovered above.

But eventually sleep overcame them and they dozed off. Ricky, half asleep, heard rattling coming from the tree. He sat up in his sleeping bag. With his eyes half closed, he saw the purple ball with the silver tassel moving back and forth rattling, its luxurious silver tassel shimmering as it swayed.

Awake, Cindy asked, "What was that?"

Puzzled, Ricky answered, "The purple ball rattled all by itself."

Sleepily getting back into her sleeping bag, Cindy mumbled, "That purple ball is really weird!"

Snuggling into his sleeping bag, Ricky said, "It really is weird. Maybe it was rattling messages to a flying saucer."

They soon fell asleep and never noticed that many Christmas balls from their tree were missing.

Next morning, shaking Ricky awake, Father said, "You let down the fort, soldier. A lot of our Christmas balls were stolen last night."

Ricky was confused as he sat up and thought about what could have happened. The purple ball was not stolen. But that rattling? The ball was sending messages, that was it! Messages to the flying saucers hovering above their house!

In a daze, Ricky said, "The purple ball, Dad."

Not aware of Ricky's thinking, Father said, "No,

the purple ball was not stolen. Did you hear or see anything last night?"

Ricky replied, "Yes, Dad, about three or so in the morning I was watching the tree when I dozed off. Half asleep, I heard the ball rattling."

"Rattling?" asked Father, his eyes bulging, "Christmas balls don't rattle!"

Mother interrupted eagerly, 'Yes Daddy, this Christmas ball rattles. It has pieces of glass inside."

"Oh . . ." said Father, "Okay, so the ball rattles, what is so unusual about that?"

Ricky answered, "Because that's how it signals the flying saucer to beam up the Christmas ornaments!"

Father could not believe Ricky. He thought his son's brains had also been beamed up! Maybe Ricky had dreamed the whole thing.

Mother said softly, "Ricky had a bad night, dear, he is talking silly."

Convinced, Ricky said, "But it's true, Mom, Cindy heard it too. The purple ball is weird, Dad!"

Cindy agreed, "Yes Daddy, I heard it too!"

Father declared, "Children, I am not going to believe all this nonsense. Tonight, we all sleep downstairs and watch the tree."

Father went to work and the children stayed in the living room, watching or being watched by the big silver eye in the purple ball.

Cindy asked, "How come other trees were robbed before we got this ball?"

After thinking, Ricky answered, "There must be other rattlers out there."

Tommy, their young neighbor, came to the door and asked: "Ricky, can I come in? Last night more balls got stolen in the neighborhood."

Ricky answered, "The flying saucers sucked them out."

Puzzled, Tommy asked, "What are you saying?"

Gazing into the silver eye, Ricky said, "The purple ball with the silver tassel is the contact with the flying saucers. When it rattles, the saucers that hover above send a beam that takes the ornaments and leaves no trace. I saw everything."

"Wow!" uttered Tommy, his eyes wide open.

In a daze, the three children sat in front of the purple ball with the silver tassel, as the ball looked back at them with its single silver eye.

MISTLETOE MADNESS

* * *

Christmas Eve was upon the Ross family and thanks to Tommy's tattle-telling, all the neighbors' attention was focused on the purple ball.

Mothers were overheard saying "We went to the police, and they said there were more serious crimes to take care of."

The girls teased, "And Cindy saw the ball flying, propelled by the silver tassel!"

The fathers joked with Mr. Ross on his way home, "Hey, Matt, let the little green men take you to their leader! Ha!"

Mr. Ross was furious when he came in the house. "I am the laughingstock of the neighborhood because of that blasted purple ball!"

Concerned, Mother said, "We had better put away the purple ball."

Spitting in fury, Mr. Ross said, "Never! That weirdo ball is not going to gain on me. I will stick it out. Tonight we wait for the robbers and clear this or spend Christmas on another planet!"

Leaving the room, Mrs. Ross shook her head and rolled her eyes.

MISTLETOE MADNESS

Later that evening, Father addressed the family. "The children will sleep in the family room and Mother and I in the studio."

Ricky asked, "How about our Christmas, Dad?"

In wicked humor, motioning that the ball wouldn't hear him, Father whispered, "Your presents are in the attic. Don't worry, we will celebrate Christmas."

Ricky asked, "And that's our Christmas?"

Tired, Father answered, "You can go out and brag with your friends about flying saucers."

Since it was Christmas Eve, the children went out and spent the evening with their friends, but they felt cold and empty. When they returned home they felt unhappy, and longed for past Christmases. Cindy complained, "Some Christmas! No way!"

* * *

As the Rosses settled into their uneasy Christmas, two men stood by the curb, next to the sorriest excuse for a car. Cautiously, they walked up the hill toward where the Ross residence stood.

The man named Fritz was chubby and talked with a lisp through the cavity of a missing front tooth. The other was Reed, a frail, skinny man who was very insecure when he talked. Reed said, "Yeah man, see? This is the house, see? Yesterday our car broke down, see? But I am sure this is the one, see?"

Impatient, Fritz slapped him, "Will you thstop thsaying, thsee, thsee? Geths on my nervesth!"

Reed answered, "You asked me, see?"

Fritz ordered, "Quieth! Geth the masther keyth!"

Ready to receive another slap, Reed answered, "Key? I don't have it, see?"

Fritz remembered the key was in his back pocket but, being so chubby, he could not reach it. He asked Reed, "Can you reachth in my backth pocketth for meth?"

Reed fumbled in Fritz's back pocket without finding any key. He said, "See? No master key, see?"

Fritz's patience ran out. He slapped him around as he exclaimed, "Thstop thsaying thsee, thsee, thsee!"

In the struggle, the key fell from Fritz's front pocket and when Reed knelt down to pick it up Fritz tumbled over Reed and both went rolling downhill. Fritz stopped rolling and Reed bumped into him. There was a lot of slapping around between them until they got up. Key in hand, Reed said, "See? I have the key, see?"

Fritz, pawing the key, grunted, "Give me thath!"

271

MISTLETOE MADNESS

Arguing in muffled voices, they approached the window. There it was, the purple ball with the silver tassel, looking back at them from the middle of the tree that stood next to the darkened fireplace.

In awe, Reed said, "See it, Fritz? The purple ball, see? I see it, see?"

Hypnotized by the silver eye, Fritz said, "Yeah, Reed, I thsee it, thsee it, thsee it, these . . ."

With a dumb smile, Reed mumbled "Oh, Fritz, see? You don't have to say 'see', 'see', 'see' I said see because I always say see, see?"

Snapping from the spell, Fritz slapped him hard. Straightening his dirty, wrinkled, white suit, he said, "Leth's getsh tho workth. You cover meth."

Using the master key, Fritz entered the house and walked to the tree. He moved to grab the purple ball, but to his surprise the ball jumped back and went sliding toward the darkened fireplace.

Fritz, not waiting for explanations, lost his composure. He ran to the fireplace fast enough to see the purple ball sliding up the chimney, onto the roof, and out of his reach. Fritz, as chubby as he was, got stuck in the fireplace and struggled to get out kicking and fussing and

272

making all kinds of noises. Mr. Ross, who had been awakened by the noise, fell on him, and Mrs. Ross started to hit him with the mop.

The ruckus woke the children, who were astonished when they saw the purple ball fall from the roof onto the front yard, and slide downhill through the grass, its silver tassel dragging behind it like a tail.

The children ran down the hill after the purple ball when they noticed the other robber, Reed, running after the ball.

Meanwhile, at the house, Mr. Ross was screaming "Amanda, call the police while I tie him up!"

Fritz pleaded with Mrs. Ross, "Don'th hith me withthe mopth, lady, the ball thslid by ithself up the chimney, I didn't thsteal ith!"

Mr. Ross had heard enough about weirdo balls for the day, so he asked Fritz, "You say that ball slid by itself up the chimney and onto the roof?"

Fritz desperately cried, "I thswear ith's the thwuth!"

Mr. Ross snorted, "Next you'll say a flying saucer sucked it out of the house!"

To save face, Fritz screamed, "Yeah, that'sth

whath happenedth!"

Mr. Ross, having enough of flying saucers, balls, and crooks, asked in exasperation, "Why, pray tell, were you after the ball?"

Fritz held his breath, making his chubby cheeks puff, his ears stick out, and his eyes bulge.

At this moment, Mrs. Ross called from the phone, "Matt, the police is on the phone."

When Matt came to the phone, the events of the day ran through his mind like a movie on fast forward. He said, "I am reporting the robbery of a flying saucer, no! A one-eyed flying ball, no! A crook that came to steal a purple ball that rattles messages to flying saucers!"

Mrs. Ross anxiously called for his attention, "Matt, you are talking crazy!"

Mr. Ross clearly heard the officer on the other end of the line saying to someone else, "Hey Mulligan, listen to this one, a real Christmas cuckoo!"

Mr. Ross, gaining his composure, cleared his throat and said, "Sorry officer, things are crazy here, I feel like I am in a loony bin. I am Mr. Matt Ross, reporting a robbery at my house on 3309 Whitepine. Please hurry!"

Cindy and Ricky went after the runaway purple

ball with its silver tassel dragging behind when they saw Reed also running after the purple ball.

Both jumped on Reed, who easily fell to the ground. Reed soon overcame them and scrambled, trying to run, when he tripped on an abandoned surfboard. Reed, as light as he was, bolted from the surfboard, smashed into a hollow tree stump at the bottom of the hill, and landed flat on his back, unconscious.

When this happened, the brittle, hollow stump ripped open under the smashing weight of Reed's body, giving way to dozens of Christmas balls.

A small, shy voice which could barely be heard, said, "That man smashed Ogger to the ground, that's good! Ogger is dead, that's good! Good!"

The children could not believe their eyes. A tiny fairy was among the Christmas balls. Pointing to the balls, Ricky asked, "Who are you? And those are the missing balls!"

The fairy said, "My name is Flashy, and Ogger was our mean, ugly Master. He wanted to accumulate Christmas balls to smash the Upper Level Fairies. He wanted their territory. Fairies can be smashed even by a Christmas ball, so he made us steal your ornaments."

MISTLETOE MADNESS

The children didn't understand and asked. "The Upper Level Fairies, are they mean to you?"

By now, many fairies were joining Flashy. They chorused, "Oh, no, we want to be friends with the Inner Earth Fairies! It was Ogger that wanted to smash us, but instead he got smashed. Good!"

Understanding, Cindy said, "So you were stealing our balls, and you were the ones that carried the purple ball out here. We thought the purple ball had magic!"

Eagerly, Flashy apologized, "We didn't want to steal the balls, honest! Ogger made us, otherwise he would punish us. Sorry."

Cindy understood and asked, "Where is my purple ball?"

Flashy rummaged among the balls and found it. He lifted it up for Cindy saying, "Glad to return your purple ball. I almost took it last night, but your brother was watching and I had to leave."

Reed regained consciousness. In one jump, he grabbed the ball from Flashy's hand and went running downhill to the curb.

Now the house was surrounded by police cars and neighbors. At the bottom of the hill there was another police car. A policeman jumped out of the car pursuing Reed. Other officers blocked Reed's run at the curb and soon Reed was in their custody.

When they got back to the house they had to break their way through neighbors and other police officers.

Mr. and Mrs. Ross were by the Christmas tree. One of the officers asked the other officer coming in, "What do you bring here, Mulligan?"

Putting the purple ball on the mantle, Mulligan said, "This fellow was running away with this purple ball."

When Fritz saw the ball, he squealed, "That the spooky ball!"

Reed cut in, "Sure, the ball jumped, see? From the chimney to the roof and to the front yard, see? Its tail dragging behind, see? I ran after it, see?"

Fritz, foaming at the mouth cried, "Freaky ballth! Letme outta hereth!"

But Reed, gaining attention, went on, "See Fritz, see? I got the ball, see? Took it from some little critter, see? They stole the Christmas balls, see?"

Officer Mulligan raised his hands and exclaimed, "Will somebody talk some sense here?"

277

MISTLETOE MADNESS

Ricky, who was avidly following the discussion, cut in excitedly, "They were fairies, not critters. They took the Christmas balls so Ogger could smash the Upper Level Fairies with them. Flashy is the fairy who gave us the purple ball!"

Confusion took over. Fritz was tied up, squirming and screaming. Reed was insistent about critters, Ricky was talking about fairies, and the neighbors were screaming to each other about who was right or wrong. The officers tried to calm everybody.

Mr. Ross was drenched in perspiration and his eyes were bulging in excitement. He yelled above the screams, "Officer Mulligan, this is out of control. Do something!"

The officers agreed, so they went out to their cars in the driveway and turned on the police siren at full blast. Everybody went silent at once. Officer Mulligan returned to the house and, lifting the purple ball from the mantel, its silver tassel spilling through his fingers, he asked, "Mr. Ross, is this your Christmas ball?"

Mr. Ross, trying his best to stay composed, managed to say, "Yes, it is ours. My wife bought it at Maxmall."

MISTLETOE MADNESS

Noticing the rattle in the ball, Mulligan unhooked the cap of the ball and shook it upside down in the hollow of his hand as he said, "This fellow Reed was running away with it. Bet he wanted something inside this ball."

In the last shakes, two diamond stones dropped into his hand.

"Ah, ha!" exclaimed Officer Mulligan. "These are the diamonds that were stolen at the Maxmall Shopping Center. No wonder we could not find them on any suspects."

Mrs. Ross blurted, "Oh, Matt, and I bought the purple ball!"

Putting a protective arm over her shoulder, Mr. Ross said, "It is over now, dear."

Mr. Ross, still puzzled, asked Officer Mulligan, "Tell me, Officer Mulligan, how do you explain the purple ball sliding from the tree, up the chimney, to the roof, jumping into the yard and sliding downhill to the tree stump? I don't believe in fairies. What do you say?"

Officer Mulligan looked at him, then into the night and into the anxious eyes of the children. Thinking for awhile, he said, "I have seen stranger things happening during Christmas nights, Mr. Ross. Leave it to Christmas and be happy. You got your purple ball back and we got back the diamonds. That makes my Christmas, so, have a very Merry Christmas everybody!"

As Fritz and Reed were taken away in officer Mulligan's police car, the two still went on arguing on the critters, fairies and freaky balls. By now, none of the police officers paid attention to their bickering as the officers got into their cars and left.

The neighbors milling on the front yard talked among themselves, "It is already Christmas, let's bring our goodies to the Ross family and let's all celebrate together. It's been hard on them. They deserve a good Christmas!"

As the Ross family rested in front of the Christmas tree, Mr. Martin, speaking for all the neighbors, stood at the door saying, "Matt and Amanda, we, know all the stress you have been through. We want to give you our support."

Giving way to the neighbors behind him, they entered the Ross's living room singing Christmas carols and carrying trays with hams, salads, cheeses, sweets and wines,. The house came alive with singing, cheers, and happiness. There was a real Christmas Spirit of sharing.

MISTLETOE MADNESS

While the adults celebrated inside, outside all the children in the neighborhood gathered and decided to look for their Christmas balls. As they picked up their balls, Cindy asked Flashy, "How come I never saw you before?"

Talking for all the fairies, Flashy said, "We are Christmas Fairies and we come out during Christmas. Always share in the Spirit of Christmas and you will see us."

Ricky asked, "Can we come and visit you?"

Flashy answered, "Come to the hollow tree stump; we live under it. We will be glad to share with you many other Christmases!"

By now, all the children had picked up their balls and said together, "Merry Christmas, dear fairies, see you next year!"

The fairies answered, "Remember to share in the Christmas Spirit, and we will celebrate together!"

They all returned to their parents, who by now were going back home after much celebrating. It was already Christmas Day. Happiness was abundant in the Ross family as they celebrated and shared their own Christmas.

From the middle of the Christmas tree, with its

silvery gaze, watching the merriment, was the purple Christmas ball with the silver tassel.

Velia M. Rolff

MISTLETOE MADNESS

Illustration by Regina Kubelka

283

What a Find

"Just one more Christmas gift to buy," said Tyler's mother, steering him towards the women's blouses.

Tyler groaned and rolled his eyes.

"You wouldn't want us to skip Auntie Sue, would you?" she added, pushing him past rows of blouses.

Bored with holiday shopping, Tyler slumped down until he was sprawled out on the floor, peering beneath the racks. A crumpled dollar bill lay just beyond his reach under the center of the rack. Tyler scooted over to grab it, smoothing it open as he stood up.

"Whoa," he said, examining the bill.

"Brush the dust off your pants, Tyler," said his mother, glancing over her shoulder with the chosen shiny

284

red blouse in hand. "We're finally done."

Tyler took a quick look around, astounded at his good fortune, and then followed his mother to the cash registers. His heart raced as he pocketed the bill. *Findsies keepsies losies weepsies.* This was no dollar bill, he had realized, but $100! More than enough for one of those new video games he'd been wanting.

Who could have put it there? he wondered. Probably some rich guy whose pockets were so full it just slipped out. Somebody so rich, they didn't even notice it was missing.

"Jingle Bells" blared from the store's speaker system. Tyler fidgeted as his mother collected her bags from the cashier, a tall woman wearing a red felt cap.

Then they headed out into the chilly air, past a bell-ringing Santa, to the car. Tyler tossed up his hood against the biting wind, glad for once to have it. He thought of the homeless people he had seen last summer when he had gone into the city to watch a baseball game, and wondered if they had coats now. Maybe someone poor had lost the money in his pocket. Not likely. As they got into the car, Tyler's stomach began to feel funny. Whoever had lost the money had probably earned it and probably wanted it back.

"Mom," Tyler said, "Is there a Lost and Found in that store?"

"Well, there's Customer Service. Did you lose something, Tyler?" she asked, starting to put the key in the ignition.

"No, I found something."

Two minutes later they were waiting in line at Customer Service. Even though Tyler's mother kept glancing at her watch, Tyler was glad he had insisted on coming back in. His stomach was starting to feel better already. And who knew, maybe there would be a big reward!

"If no one claims this, we'll give you a call," said the clerk, slipping the money into an envelope.

The next evening, as Tyler was putting a few last ornaments on the tree, the telephone rang. He heard his mother answer, "Yes. my son found the money."

Tyler's eyes got wide as he ran off to make a final decision from his game catalog. "Yes!" he whispered, slamming his fist in the air.

"Tyler," his mother called, a moment later.

"I know," Tyler shouted, running into the kitchen

with his catalog.

"It's the woman who lost the money," whispered his mother still holding the phone. "She wants to talk to you."

"Oh," said Tyler, closing his catalog and reaching for the phone. "Hello?"

"I am *so* thankful to you," said a woman's voice, "That money you found was all the money I had left to buy groceries and Christmas gifts for my children. I nearly panicked when I realized it wasn't in my purse. I was sure it had been stolen. Then my son suggested I ask at Customer Service." She paused to take a breath.

"You're welcome," said Tyler.

"I'd like you to have $10 of it as a thank you."

"No, that's okay," said Tyler.

After the call, Tyler tossed the game catalog under his bed and tried to feel happy about turning in the money. Somehow the brightly lit Christmas tree didn't look as stunning now. He peered into a gold Christmas ornament and scowled at his distorted reflection.

The next day, out on the school playground, Tyler still felt down in the dumps. All the kids were talking about what they wanted for Christmas.

MISTLETOE MADNESS

"What do you think you'll get for Christmas?" asked his friend Joey, rubbing his hands together in the frosty air.

Tyler shrugged his shoulders. "I don't know. Probably a video game." He thought a minute. "I'm having trouble getting into the ho ho ho business this year."

"Well, I can't wait!" shouted Joey, running off to talk to someone else.

Then a kid from a lower grade came up to Tyler. Snow was beginning to fall and Tyler wondered what was wrong with him. *Where was his jacket?* The boy's sweatshirt had a hole in it and his pants were too short, but his eyes were bright as he looked up at Tyler with a look Tyler hadn't seen before. The kind of look Tyler's friends would save for their sports heroes.

"Are you the kid who turned in the money?" the boy asked shyly.

Tyler glanced around wondering if the whole school knew, then he nodded.

"Thanks," said the boy gazing up at him, "that was my Mom who lost it."

Tyler swallowed hard as finally a burst of holiday

joy rose from deep inside him. "Merry Christmas," he managed.

Marcia Strykowski

My Special Part

"What I want for Christmas, 1937," I wrote on my tablet. Underneath, I began my list with "red dress." Daddy told me we were in a state of depression and not to expect much this year. I didn't know what the state of depression was, but I knew that I would really be depressed if I didn't get a good part in the Christmas program.

Last week I'd bragged to Grandma Johnson about the special part I had. She surprised me by promising that she and Grandpa would come to watch me perform. The truth was, I hadn't yet been assigned a part.

Last year I was queen in that play about bringing gifts to the Christchild. I didn't have much to say, but I liked being all dressed up. My line was, "I will lay my crown upon the altar." Of course, what happened before that was embarrassing. I must have been too close to the edge of the stage because, when the curtain was raised, it grabbed the bottom of my robe. Miss Hogan called, "Lower the curtain." She whispered to me, "Elizabeth, stand back a bit." From then on my part went well. I just knew she'd picked out something special for me this year.

I shoved my spelling book and tablet under my desk and hopped up to get in line. Mrs. Rosella's class had already gone downstairs for the rehearsal. The racket sounded like bedlam, whatever that was supposed to be. But when we got down there, Miss Hogan, my teacher, quieted everybody down in a hurry.

The first and second graders were first, each one carrying a bell as they walked up on stage. They needed help with their verses, but this was only the first practice. They ended their part by ringing the bells and singing "Jingle Bells."

The eighth grade boys arranged the scenery for the third and fourth graders' play. This is where the problem began.

"We need more elves," Mrs. Rosella announced.

MISTLETOE MADNESS

"Elizabeth Johnson, you're the right size. Come on up here."

I couldn't believe it. An elf? Just because I was the shortest in my room! I wanted a special part and that didn't include an elf.

"Up here." Mrs. Rosella tapped her foot on the floor. "We haven't got all day. Now, let's get on with the rehearsal."

All five of us elves stood on benches in the back looking stupid, not even doing elf things. The play was something about the night before Christmas, otherwise known as Christmas Eve.

Next came a play put on by my class. I hadn't been given a part in that, but I kept hoping. After the plays, came tryouts for the musical parts. Maybe Miss Hogan had a musical part picked out for me.

Harold played the piano. The twins, Leona and Leon, sang a duet. Richard tried to play his violin, but it squeaked worse than it does when I run my fingernails down the blackboard.

"Thank you, Richard," Mrs. Rosella said. "We have room for one more musical number."

I squeezed my eyes tight and whispered, "Please,

MISTLETOE MADNESS

Jesus, let her call on me."

"Christine."

I sighed. Christine was a seventh grader, and she usually sang something when we had talent time. So it was only natural that she'd be called on to sing.

Christine looked so pretty as she sang "Jolly Old St. Nicholas." Her father must not have been depressed because she owned the prettiest red dress. I'd even invited her home from school with me once, just so Mama could see the dress and get me one like it. But Mama said I didn't have the figure for it. Christine was tall and thin with long shiny black hair, and she filled out the dress in just the right places. My short pudgy body would fill it out in all the wrong places. Mama was right.

"Do we have any more volunteers?" Miss Hogan asked.

My hand shot straight up in the air.

Miss Hogan said, "Okay, Elizabeth, you try it."

I nearly tripped over my own feet as I ran up on stage. Mrs. Rosella gave me an introduction and I began. "Jolly old St. Nicholas, lean your rear this . . ."

A couple of little kids in the front row were whispering and giggling. Were they laughing at me? What did I do wrong? Was my dress pulled up to show my underwear? Mrs. Rosella took her eyes off the music and hit a wrong note. I lost my place and couldn't get started again.

"I think we'll let Christine sing," Mrs. Rosella said. "We need you for an elf."

My eyeballs burned and my throat felt choked as I tried not to cry. It was all her fault. When the kids acted up, she hit the wrong note and threw me off. Mrs. Rosella never liked me anyway when I was in her class. If only I didn't have to wear sackcloth—that's what Daddy called my dresses that Mama made out of feedbags. Daddy said money was scarcer than hen's teeth. He ought to know, about the teeth I mean; he raised chickens. There just wasn't enough money for a new red dress, and feedbags didn't come in red.

School let out at noon the day of our Christmas program. I ran upstairs to change out of my school clothes and couldn't believe what I found. There, across my bed, lay a red dress. I picked it up carefully. Where did it come from?

Mama stood in the doorway. "Do you like it?"

When I was able to talk, I said, "I love it. Where in

the . . ."

"Grandma gave me a piece of cloth to make myself a dress. Red dye costs only a few pennies, and I knew how disappointed you were not to get a better part in the program. So this is an early Christmas present."

It had been a long time since Mama had a new dress, and I knew she really needed one. I threw my arms around Mama's neck. A tear rolled down my cheek, and then another.

Mama's voice cracked as she said, "Now, don't go and cry."

That night I proudly wore my new red dress, not like Christine's, but just right for me. I looked around the room to see if Christine wore hers, too, but didn't see her.

The program went smoothly. The little ones did a good job with their jingle bell part. Richard didn't play his violin, but the twins sang "Up On The Housetop." Harold played "Santa Claus Is Coming To Town" while the stage was getting ready; then we were on with our play.

Christine was supposed to be next, but she hadn't shown up yet. I slid out of my elf costume and went back to sit with my class.

Just before the end of the play by the upper grades,

MISTLETOE MADNESS

Miss Hogan came over to me. She whispered, "Elizabeth, you wanted to sing. Do you know the song well enough to sing it? Christine is ill and couldn't come."

Did I know the song? I'd been driving my family nuts with that jolly old man. What if I got mixed up again? Certainly the little kids wouldn't laugh at me this time. Miss Hogan was waiting.

Suddenly, I knew what had bothered me about this whole Christmas program. It wasn't just that I didn't get a special part, but that Christ had been left out.

I nodded. "Could my mother play for me?"

She hesitated, and then agreed.

I went back to find my mother and whispered in her ear. She understood.

As soon as the clapping stopped, Miss Hogan announced, "Tonight we have left to the end a very special number by Elizabeth Johnson."

It will be special, I thought. As I walked up on stage in my red dress, I thought of Christine. I felt tall and slim with dark hair, rather than mousy brown. I looked over the audience until I found Grandma sitting in the back. Mom took her seat at the piano and began to play, but it wasn't "Jolly Old St. Nicholas"—that was

MISTLETOE MADNESS

Christine's song.

"Joy to the world, the Lord is come," I began and sang with my whole heart.

I'd done it. It wasn't the right song for the program, but I'd let everyone know the reason for Christmas.

Marion Tickner

Joshua Was There:
A Shepherd's Guide to the Holy Night

It was a typical winter night in the hill country of Judea. The air was crisp and the sky was as dark as a moonless starlit night could be. The sheep were down for the night, but the shepherds stood watch, protecting their charges from marauding animals set on a quick meal of lamb. It was a continual contest between the shepherds and the wolves, bears and lions. Somewhere over by the outcropping of rocks, a shepherd was singing to his sheep, to help them settle down for the night.

The youngest shepherd was a boy just a year or

two older than you. His name was Joshua and this was his first experience as a shepherd in the hill country. He was herding with his older brother to oversee the family flock. As a beginner, he had charge of only one lamb. He was very proud of his lamb, a gift from his father. He was pleased to be old enough to be a shepherd and be entrusted with the care of the flock.

The shepherds huddled around the fire when it was not their turn to guard the flocks. It was just as Joshua returned to the fire, from checking the flock, that there was a commotion in the sky. Joshua was blinded by a sudden flash of light in the midnight sky. When his eyes adjusted to the light, he saw a person in the center of the circle of light. The person was wearing a white robe bound with gold cords. Joshua was frightened until he heard the being speak. What a beautiful loving voice he heard; Joshua felt love sweeping over him all the time the angel was speaking. For Joshua had decided the being was an angel when he saw its wings.

Joshua was so busy taking in every detail of the angel, he didn't hear anything the angel said. The next thing he knew there were more angels. There were so many angels he couldn't even count them, and they were singing "Glory to God" and things like that. When they left, Joshua was in a daze. He'd never had anything like that happen before. He didn't realize it, but nothing like that had happened to any of the others, either. When Joshua came back to his senses, he heard the shepherds talking about going to Bethlehem to see whatever it was the angel had told them about.

Joshua told his brother he was going to go to Bethlehem with the older shepherds.

"What about your responsibility for your lamb?" his brother asked.

Joshua told his brother to take care of his lamb. Joshua was determined to go to Bethlehem with the other shepherds, even if it meant his brother had to stay behind.

The way to Bethlehem was long, but the shepherds didn't notice. They were too busy recounting the angel and its message.

When they reached the village, it was easy to find the stable where the baby was sleeping in the manger. They told Mary and Joseph how they had learned about the baby. Mary and Joseph were amazed at what the shepherds told them.

After seeing the baby, the shepherds returned to

the hill country and to their flocks. It was against the nature of the normally solitary men, but they were so excited that they talked all the way back, praising and glorifying God for all they had seen and heard. But Joshua was very quiet. He considered everything he had heard and treasured it all in his heart. It all affected him greatly. Just seeing the baby made Joshua realize how selfish he had been when he left his brother to tend all of the sheep. His brother would have felt good just seeing the baby, as Joshua had. Joshua decided he would take his brother to Bethlehem. He worked out his plan on the way back to the hill country.

As the group returned to the fire ring, Joshua went to one of the older shepherds and asked if he would watch his brother's flock. The older shepherd was still so excited by the holy experience that he was eager to help in any way.

Joshua approached his lamb, picked up the little ewe and placed her across his shoulders, while calling to his brother, "Benjamin, come. I need your help. Go with me to Bethlehem."

Benjamin answered, "You just got back. Why are you going again?"

MISTLETOE MADNESS

Joshua answered vaguely," Oh, I just have something I want to do."

But Benjamin sensed what Joshua was going to do when Joshua joined him on the path with his lamb across his shoulders. He asked earnestly, "Do you have your lamb with you for a reason?"

Joshua answered "yes," in a voice that implied Benjamin was to stop asking questions.

"Are you going to do what I think you are going to do?"

Joshua replied, "It depends on what you think I am going to do."

Benjamin protested, "That little ewe is the beginning of your future flock. It is the basis of your whole future. Without that lamb you will never have your own flock. You will have to work to build someone else's fortune all of your life."

Joshua responded, "Wait till you meet the baby. You will understand. I just feel I can trust him with my very life and everything I have. When I stood there by the manger I knew that I could trust him with my heart, my livelihood, with everything I am."

Benjamin sensed there was no point trying to

302

change Joshua's mind, so the older brother and Joshua continued on their journey, silently. When they got to Bethlehem, they went directly to the stable.

As Benjamin experienced the presence of the baby, he understood how Joshua felt. He gave his little brother a squeeze and said, "I am so grateful you brought me to see this wonderful baby."

Before they left Joshua took the lamb from his shoulders saying, "Please take this for the baby. I want him to have my lamb."

As Joseph accepted the lamb for baby Jesus, a small tear escaped from his eye and made its way down his cheek, for he recognized the sacrifice Joshua was making.

Ardeen Fredrick

MISTLETOE MADNESS

Illustration by Elizabeth O. Dulemba

The Clauses Go Hollywood

Mr. and Mrs. Santa Claus gathered around their fireplace on a cold, North Pole night. Santa painted toys for the children. Mrs. Claus knitted mittens for the elves. As long as Santa was working, he was happy. But Mrs. Claus didn't seem her usual cheerful self.

"Is everything all right, Ma-Ma?" Santa asked.

Mrs. Claus shrugged her shoulders. "Everything's fine," she said.

"Now, Ma-Ma, don't give me that," said Santa. "I can tell when something's bothering you."

Mrs. Claus dropped her knitting needles into her lap. "It's just that we're always doing things for everyone else, Pa-Pa. I wish that, just once, we could do something

305

for ourselves."

"I do too sometimes, Ma-Ma," said Santa. "But everyone depends on us so much."

There was a loud knock at the door.

"We'll finish this talk later," Santa said. He walked over and opened the door.

Outside, stood a sort of odd-looking fellow. He wore a flashy, pin-striped suit. He had a thin, greasy mustache. "Aren't you folks gonna invite me in?" he asked. "It's chillsville out here."

"Of course, come in," Santa said warmly. Before Santa even finished the sentence, the man was inside. Melting snow from the stranger's suit dripped onto the rug.

"Max Sterling's the name," said the stranger.

Mrs. Claus sprang up so fast, her ball of yarn unraveled. It rolled across the rug. "Max Sterling?" she gasped. "THE Max Sterling? The big Hollywood movie producer?"

"In the flesh," Max replied.

"What are you doing all the way up in the North Pole?" Santa asked.

Max opened his jacket. He tucked his thumbs

beneath his suspenders. "Us big-time producers get around," he said.

"Would you like some sweet potato pie?" asked Mrs. Claus.

"Never touch the stuff," said Max. He patted his flat stomach. "Gotta keep myself trim."

"Is there some special reason you've come to see us?" asked Santa.

"As a matter of fact there is," said Max. "I need some well-known faces for my next picture."

"How can we help?" asked Santa. "We're in the business of making toys."

"I'll get right to the point, folks. I want to put the two of you in the movies."

"Us?" yelled Mrs. Claus. Her glasses slid down her nose. "You want *us*?"

"Sure," said Max. "You're naturals. And who's more famous than the world famous Clauses?"

"We're *that* famous?" asked Mrs. Claus.

"Honey, you're known the world over. And I'm going to make you even bigger stars."

"Oh, my!" Mrs. Claus nervously patted her hair.

"Good. It's all settled then," said Max. "We leave

right away for the land of heaven on earth: Hollywood."

Santa scratched his head. "I don't know about this," he said. "It just doesn't seem like the right thing to do."

"Oh, please, Pa-Pa, please," begged Mrs. Claus.

Santa couldn't help but notice how thrilled his wife looked. He'd do anything to make her happy. "All right, Ma-Ma, if this is what you want."

"Yippee!" yelled Mrs. Claus. She jumped up and down. Santa hadn't seen her this excited in over one hundred years.

"I'll hitch up the reindeer," said Santa.

"Wait, wait, you're with me, old buddy," said Max. "We're flying in style. On a jet."

"But I always—"

"Never mind what you always used to do, old boy. Life is going to be very different—starting right now."

Santa shrugged his shoulders. "All right. If it makes Ma-Ma happy . . ."

The ride to Hollywood seemed endless. They changed planes so many times that Santa stopped counting. On the last plane, the other passengers wore t-shirts and shorts. Santa felt hot and silly in his red, woolen suit.

Finally, the plane landed. Max whisked Santa and Mrs. Claus over to the ritzy Hollywood Hotel. On their way to the room, they passed the pool. Everyone lounged around wearing dark sunglasses and tight bathing suits. "Get a look at those old folks in the funny suits," someone yelled.

"Don't worry about those jerks," said Max. "We'll have you fixed up in no time."

"Fixed up?" asked Santa. "What do you mean by that?"

Max patted Santa on the back. "Trust me, old buddy. Trust me."

Max dropped Santa and Mrs. Claus off at their room. "Gotta run, folks," he said. He glanced at his watch. "I'll check back with you in a few weeks."

"A few weeks?" Mrs. Claus blurted out.

"Yeah—in the meantime, you're in good hands. Relax. Order room service. Everyone in this hotel is here to serve you." Max left quickly. The Clauses sat there for a few minutes, staring at each other. Then they realized they were hungry. They might as well order room service. But their turkey dinner with sweet potato pie never arrived. The hotel waiter brought them grapefruit juice and carrot sticks instead.

"Just following Mr. Sterling's orders," said the waiter.

Then a woman from the hotel dragged the Clauses upstairs to the gym. She made them exercise for hours. "Just following Mr. Sterling's orders," said the woman.

For two weeks the Clauses exercised every day and ate mostly carrots and celery. They felt sore and dizzy and weak.

Finally Max showed up again. "I see dieting agrees with you folks." Max handed Mrs. Claus a skimpy black dress. It glittered. "I'll bet you can slip into this now, doll," Max said. He rubbed his greasy mustache.

Mrs. Claus stared at the black dress. "Gracious! It really *is* special."

"I'm sending a gal over to help you get beautiful," said Max.

"Wait a minute now, my wife is already beautiful," Santa insisted.

"Yeah, yeah," said Max. "You know that, and I know it . . . but we could all use a little help. You get my drift?"

MISTLETOE MADNESS

Max grabbed Santa by the arm. "Let's leave the little lady alone now to fix herself up. Us men need to talk business down by the pool."

At pool side, Max and Santa sat in oversized lounge chairs. "Do we have to sit out here?" Santa asked. He rubbed his chin. "It's kind of hot. Especially with this beard."

"Well, old boy, this is your lucky day. Today is the day that beard is going to go."

"Go? Go where?" Santa asked.

"You know, like—shaven. Gone. Removed from your face forever."

Santa clenched his beard. "I've had these whiskers for as long as I can remember."

"You wanna be a big movie star, don't you, Santa?" asked Max.

"I . . . I guess. If it's still what Ma-Ma wants."

Max slapped Santa on the back. "Do it for *her*," he said. By the way, your glasses are history too."

"What? I can't see anything without my glasses."

"We'll fix you up with contact lenses. In the meantime, wear these." Max handed Santa a pair of black sunglasses.

MISTLETOE MADNESS

Santa carefully took off his glasses and put on the sunglasses. He could hardly see anything. All around him he heard strange noises.

"What's going on?" he asked.

"Those clown movie stars are just whistling at some babe."

Santa stared through the dark sunglasses. He thought he saw a young blonde woman. She wore a tight black dress and high heels.

"Wow!" Santa exclaimed. "Is she a big Hollywood star?"

"She will be very soon," said Max. "But don't pay attention to her now."

Santa couldn't stop watching. It looked like the poor woman was wobbly in her high heels. Maybe she felt dizzy in the hot sun.

Max shoved a stack of papers under Santa's nose. "Just sign this little contract," he said. "Then you and the Mrs. will be set for life."

Suddenly Santa heard a big splash! The woman had tumbled head first into the pool.

"HEELLP!!" she screeched.

"That's Ma-Ma's voice," hollered Santa. "She

can't swim."

Santa jumped up to rescue her. All the male movie stars jumped up too.

"What a babe," hollered Guy Mallone.

"I saw her first," yelled Tadd Britt.

In the mad rush to the pool, the movie stars trampled Santa. His sunglasses popped off. He hit his head on the concrete and passed out.

An hour later, he woke up. He was in his hotel room, in bed. Mrs. Claus was in the bed next to his. Her arms were black and blue.

"Are you all right?" Santa asked.

"Thank goodness you're awake," said Mrs. Claus. You really had me worried."

"Are you all right?" Santa repeated. "What's wrong with your arm?"

"There were so many movie stars pulling at me. Imagine, Guy Mallone and Tadd Britt fighting over me."

"You're not hurt are you?" asked Santa.

"Hurt? I've never been so thrilled in my life," said Mrs. Claus.

"That's nice," Santa said. But he was sad. He closed his eyes. His head ached. He didn't want to look at his wife's blurry blonde hair. Maybe the movie stars liked her new look, but Santa didn't. He thought she looked skinny and pale.

"We got a phone call from home today, Pa-Pa," said Mrs. Claus. "The elves are having production problems."

"That's too bad," said Santa. "A lot of children will be disappointed this Christmas."

"I've been thinking a lot about that," said Mrs. Claus.

Santa opened his eyes. "You have?"

"Well . . . thanks to you I've had the time of my life. I could never have imagined anything this exciting happening to me."

Santa lowered his head.

"But I think I've had enough excitement to keep me happy for a lifetime," said Mrs. Claus.

"Do you mean it?" Santa asked.

"Would you mind if we went home now?" asked Mrs. Claus.

"No. Of course not," said Santa. "But what about Max?"

"I'll explain it to him," said Mrs. Claus. "Even

314

MISTLETOE MADNESS

Max was a little boy once."

"Oh, Ma-Ma, you've made me so happy," said Santa. There were tears in his eyes. Suddenly, Santa sprung up in bed and grabbed his chin. "Ahh, thank goodness," he said. "I still have my beard."

Karen Ann Carpenter

Thoughts of Happiness

Sunshine and daisies have disappeared
Nothing to greet God's only Son
But still we meet every year
To celebrate only One.

But what happens to those who don't know
And those who have never cared
To hear about this Son of God
Will they never get their share?

I won't answer these questions
No, no I won't, I can't
This is a life-learned lesson
Not one learned in a second

MISTLETOE MADNESS

So if you're hoping for happiness
Look up to the skies
'Cause He's with your guardian angel
Be happy 'cause He's alive!

Lucia de León

MISTLETOE MADNESS

Illustration by Terri L. Sanders

A Christmas Tree for Emily

Emily remembered well the Christmas when she was seven. It was 1943, and the United States was at war.

Emily's family, along with all the other people they knew in their small town, had been issued ration stamps by the Government. Whenever the wanted to buy something such as coffee, sugar, butter, gasoline, automobile tires, shoes, or chocolate, they had to have ration stamps in addition to paying with money. About two weeks before Christmas, Emily and her mother were seated at the breakfast table for several minutes before her father joined them.

"I'm afraid there is some bad news in the paper this morning," Emily's father said, after taking a sip from his coffee cup. "Unfortunately, we're not going to be able to have a Christmas tree this year . . ."

"Why not?" Emily asked, interrupting her father before he was through speaking.

"Well, because so many men are away fighting in the war, there are not enough experienced workers to help cut the trees. And the trucks can't get enough gasoline to bring the trees all the way to Texas from Canada.

"It won't seem much like Christmas without a tree," Emily's mother said. We'll just have to . . ."

Emily interrupted again, trying hard to blink back the tears. "But we'll still get to have presents, won't we?"

"Of course there'll be some presents. And a special Christmas dinner, too. You know, I've been saving some extra sugar stamps, so I'll even be able to make some candy this year," Emily's mother said, trying to console her.

Emily's father rose from the table, kissed his wife on the forehead, then kneeled down by Emily's chair. "Honey, there'll be lots of lights on the big tree in the town square, so it will just have to be our tree this year." He wiped her tears with his handkerchief, then hugged her and hurried off to work.

MISTLETOE MADNESS

During recess at school later that day, Emily and her friends giggled and talked about their Christmas wishes and holiday plans. Some of the children's parents had also told them about the scarcity of trees, while others were hearing about it for the first time. Some of them were crying as they went back inside to their classroom.

Then one day shortly before Christmas, Emily's father came home earlier than usual. He beamed with pride as he opened the trunk of the car and removed a small pine tree he had cut from a friend's pasture on the outskirts of town. Unlike spruce or fir trees, pine trees have thin branches and long prickly needles, which make them hard to decorate. But not wanting to disappoint him, Emily and her mother did their best to make the tree presentable by using all of the decorations they owned— one string of twelve multicolored lights, a few glass ornaments, and some icicles.

"I bet we're the only ones in the whole town who have a tree," Emily announced as she danced around and around with excitement.

The following morning, Emily opened the back door to let her cat, Mitzi, inside. The cat ran straight into the living room and quickly climbed to the top of the tree.

MISTLETOE MADNESS

Before Emily or her mother could stop it, the tree toppled, breaking all of the lights and ornaments as it hit the floor. Her mother became angry and chased the cat out of the house with a broom. Emily burst into tears, crying not only about the tree, but because her mother said Mitzi would never be allowed in the house again.

As they cleaned up the broken glass and set the tree upright, Emily and her mother talked about possible ways to redecorate the tree. Because of the war shortage and their lack of money, there could be no new lights or ornaments.

The next day when Emily came home from school, they worked well into the night making paper chains from multicolored construction paper, stringing popcorn and cranberries. Using cookie cutters for patterns, aluminum foil from gum wrappers glued onto cardboard became bells, stars, and moons. They tied bows on the branches using ribbons her mother had saved from boxes of candy and stationery. A few apples and oranges, dotted with nutmeg, were hung on the lower branches.

Many Christmases have passed since then, but each December when Emily closes her eyes, she sees the sad little tree in her family's living room window. It

322

MISTLETOE MADNESS

shines more brightly than any other in her memory.

Carol J. Rhodes

Piney's Special Christmas

Piney Jones was looking forward to the Christmas holidays. He really liked living on the farm and helping his Uncle Nate, but he missed his daddy. His daddy had given him the strange nickname he had always gone by. His habit of chewing on a pine needle caused everyone to call him Piney now instead of Milton James, a name he really hated anyway.

Piney's dad worked out of town most of the time and this year the red-haired boy wanted a big, nice tree and a special present for his mama. Last year, all he had gotten her was his homemade sage brooms.

"Uncle Nate, let's have a really big tree this year. Last year everybody was a little sad on account of Daddy's

MISTLETOE MADNESS

job."

"Yep, your Pa has a good job now, Piney. Let's hope it lasts. Don't do a man no good to be out of a job."

"I just wish I could think of somethin' special for Mama."

"She'll appreciate anythin', Piney."

"I know that . . . hot dog! I got it! Piney raced to the house.

He rummaged around in his mother's closet, got what he wanted, took the money his daddy had given him for his mama's present and started out the door.

"Where are you goin', Piney?"

"Uncle Nate needs some tobacco, Mama. I thought I'd go to town and get it for him."

"You up to a little polishin' since it's so close to Christmas?"

"No'm, just doin' him a favor."

"All right, be careful."

Piney scampered on down the road toward town. After he left, Uncle Nate came in the house for a drink.

"I see Piney's shinin' up to you, since it's close to Christmas."

"What are you talkin' about?" Nate asked.

MISTLETOE MADNESS

"He went to town after your tobacco, didn't he?"

"No! I'm not out of . . ." he realized he had given Piney away.

"Well, what did he go to town for?" Mrs. Jones asked.

"Don't be so nosy, Martha Nell. It's too close to Christmas!"

In the meantime Piney was in the fabric store in town.

"Mrs. Simmons, do you think Mama would like this blue?"

"I'm sure she would, Piney. This is very thoughtful of you to buy material for your mother."

"I'm goin' to have it made, too. I borrowed a dress out of her closet," he said and grinned. "It's for Mrs. Smith to use to get her size."

"This is really a special gift, Piney," laughed Mrs. Simmons.

Piney purchased the blue material and took his package over to Mrs. Smith's house.

"Mrs. Smith, do you think you could use this dress for a pattern, and make Mama a dress for Christmas?"

"Why sure, Piney. I been doin' your Mama's

sewing for years. That's such a pretty piece of cloth. Did you pick it out?"

"Yessum, I wanted to give Mama somethin' special."

"That's sweet, Piney. I'll have it ready by next weekend."

The next few days were taken up with Christmas doings at church and wrapping gifts. It was soon time for the tree to be put up.

"I want a real big tree that reaches the ceiling," announced Piney.

"Piney, whatever for?" His mother asked.

"I want a big one. We always get a little one and set it on a table. This year I want a tall one."

They got the tree and it took Uncle Nate some time to get it trimmed to fit. It didn't reach the ceiling, though, since the ceilings were about twelve feet high in the old house.

Piney had already picked up his Mama's dress, and was ready to put it under the tree.

"Now, Piney, you be careful around this tree. It's so big, it might fall over."

"I will, Mama." Piney spied Scrap, his cat,

sneaking in. Scrap was famous for getting in trouble, or rather, getting Piney trouble. Scrap had even fallen in the well once and had to be fished out with the well bucket.

"Scrap, you get out of here. You'll tear the packages."

Sure enough, Scrap headed straight for all the trailing tinsel and the ribbons on the packages.

"Scrap, I said come here!" Piney got under the tree trying to catch the cat.

Instead of coming to Piney, the cat started climbing up the tree.

Piney grabbed him, and over went the tree, right on top of Piney and the cat.

It scared Scrap so much, he ran like lightning under the couch. Piney tried to get out of the way, and a Christmas ball broke right on his head.

"Ouch, ouch!" yelled Piney, as the glass dug in his head and cedar needles scratched his arms.

"Piney! Look at this mess! I told you to stay away from that tree!"

"I was tryin' to get Scrap, Mama. He was in the tree," explained Piney, in a muffled voice from beneath the tree.

MISTLETOE MADNESS

"Let's get the tree off the boy, Martha Nell. He must be eaten up with cedar needles."

They lifted up the tree, and Piney crawled out. "It didn't break but two balls, Mama."

"I'm surprised it didn't demolish every decoration on it! Look at your head. You've got red glass all in your hair!"

The tree was righted and Piney's hair cleaned of the red glass.

"It's still a pretty tree, Mama. Wait, I got a package to put under it!

Piney got out the pretty package, and put it under the tree. He had gotten Mrs. Smith to wrap it for him, and sneaked the old dress back in the closet before his Mama missed it.

It was soon Christmas morning, and Piney could hardly wait to see if his Mama liked the blue dress.

"Here, Mama, this is from me. This year, I got you somethin' really nice. I didn't make you brooms this year."

"Piney, I really liked my brooms. Is this somethin' I need too?

"Well . . . I don't know. I just liked it."

She pulled the package open and exclaimed.

MISTLETOE MADNESS

"Piney, what a pretty dress. I love this color. Don't tell me you picked this out!"

"All by myself, and I sneaked a dress of yours for Mrs. Smith to measure by."

"You mean you had it made and everything?"

"Yessum, I sure did."

She hugged her red-haired son, and said. "Piney, you never cease to amaze me."

Piney sat looking at the fireplace and the Christmas lights on his big tree. He was glad his Mama liked the dress. It gave him a good feeling to please someone. He liked being with his family on these special days. He also enjoyed just being a child in the Deep South nearly fifty years ago.

Dorothy Baughman

Miracle on Stone Street

"You're going to watch that again?" Leeland asked.

"So what?" Liz slipped *Miracle on 34th Street* into the VCR, despite her brother's comments.

"How old are you these days? Four?"

"Lee, just stop it. I'm going to be eight in April, you know that."

"I would, if you ever acted like it. Who still believes in Santa?"

"You're ten and you act like a two year old."

Leeland reached over and flicked Liz's ear. Instead of pinching him back like she wanted to, she laughed, and tickled his tummy.

331

"What do you have against Santa?" Liz asked, still laughing.

"Nothing," Leeland said. "Just prove to me that Santa exists and I'll quit bugging you."

"Some things you can't prove, you just have to believe."

Leeland flicked Liz's ear again. "Then I still get to bug you. How does Santa do it all? What about his flying reindeer, huh?"

"Just let me watch the movie!"

"Fine." Leeland had nothing better to do, so he watched *Miracle on 34th Street* with his sister. Butch, their pet dog, jumped on the couch and slept between them. Liz ran her hand over his rough, gray fur.

"Watching that video again?" Dad asked as he walked into the living room with Mom. Butch greeted them by wagging his tail.

. "Christmas is just a couple of weeks away. Have you both thought about what presents you want?" Mom asked.

"There's a new video game out," Leeland answered.

"Liz, what about you?"

"I want something special this year, but I haven't figured it out yet."

After dinner, Mom suggested going out for pizza, so the Lucas family headed to Paul's Pizza Place.

"DAD, watch out!" Leeland screamed. A white dog with black spots ran out into the road.

"Blitz, Blitz, come back here!" yelled a white-haired man running after the dog. Dad slammed on his brakes in time. Mom and everyone in the car let out a breath of relief. The man picked up the dog and ran out of the street.

"Whew, that was a close call," Dad said.

Nobody said anything else about the incident, but Liz kept thinking about the dog and the man while she ate.

A few days later, Liz took Butch on a walk down Stone Street. A gray cat was in her neighbor's yard. Butch's gray fur stood on end, and he pulled on the leash. As she got closer, Liz realized it wasn't a cat—it was a raccoon! Butch barked like crazy, and he kept pulling and pulling. Liz lost her grip on the leash and Butch ran off.

"Butch, come back!" Liz screamed. Butch ran down Stone Street until he was out of sight. Liz searched for two hours before she finally went home to explain what happened. The Lucas family searched for Butch right away, but couldn't find him anywhere. Butch was gone.

Day after day went by, and no Butch. Leeland and Liz posted signs all over their neighborhood with information about the missing dog. Day after day, it was getting closer to Christmas.

Leeland didn't care so much about the video game and Liz couldn't even think about Christmas presents. Everyone wanted Butch home.

On Christmas Eve, Liz couldn't sleep and kept repeating, "I believe. I believe."

Christmas morning, Leeland and Liz woke up to hot chocolate and a few gifts. But there was no Butch.

"What's that sound?" Leeland asked.

"Sounds like bells," said Liz.

"It sure does," said Mom.

The Lucas family went outside. Walking down the street were nine dogs, all with bells hanging from their collars. Everyone's jaw dropped!

"Hey, that's the guy Dad almost ran over!" shouted Leeland.

"You're right! Look, he's wearing a red cap!" Liz shouted back. "And isn't that the dog that ran onto the road?" Liz asked, pointing to Blitz.

"BUTCH!" Liz and Leeland shouted together as their gray terrier ran up to greet them, his tail wagging faster than they had ever seen.

"Merry Christmas," the man said. "I found this dog recently, and then saw a poster in the neighborhood."

"You found Butch! I never thought we would see him again," Liz said. Mom and Dad hugged each other.

A yellow lab with a pink nose came over and licked Leeland's hands.

"Sorry about that," the white haired man said. "Rudy is quite a friendly dog."

"We owe you a reward," Dad said.

"You don't owe me anything. Seeing these children's faces is the best gift of all," the man said with a wink. He began to walk away quickly, Rudy leading the other seven dogs.

Liz and Leeland followed him, but when they reached the end of Stone Street, the man and the dogs were nowhere to be found.

"What are you thinking?" asked Leeland.

MISTLETOE MADNESS

"Some things you can't prove, you just have to believe." Liz felt like it was a miracle on Stone Street.

Jessica Anderson

MISTLETOE MADNESS

Illustration by Elizabeth O. Dulemba

337

Leader of the Band

He was in a trance. Through a heavy fog, he heard the crowd cheering and shouting his name. The thunder of excited feet echoed through a packed stadium as the ball whistled through the air toward him. Eric's bat splintered upon impact. He was certain he had broken records. The baseball rocketed through the frigid air and out of the ball park. Crash! The unmistakable sound of shattering glass ended the daydream and the fog gave way to a field of snow-covered asphalt.

Eric stood, with his jaw dropped open, staring at the gaping hole in the glass door of the Happy Trails retirement home. Neatly hung garlands with bright red bows were still draped across the door frame. For an instant, he thought about running away, but decided to do the right thing instead. If his grandfather had still been around, he knew what he would say. It was time to pay the fiddler. Eric sulked toward the lobby of the retirement home. His heart raced while nervousness turned his cheeks the same vibrant red as his hair. He crossed the mound of broken glass and immediately looked up to see Ms. Larsen, the plump manager of the home. She was holding one hand over her mouth and the other over her heart as if she'd just escaped a train wreck. One look at Eric's bat and she knew he had been the train. Silver tinsel and broken ornaments littered the floor at her feet where they had been dropped. She repeated the "somebody could have been hurt" speech to him and insisted that Eric call his mother. This was the third window he had broken in as many months.

"Strike three, I'm out," Eric said to himself as he began to pace.

Twenty minutes later, his mother crunched over the broken glass in the doorway and squinted her eyes at Eric, giving him that 'you're in big trouble' look that he had come to know too well.

"Mom," Eric said, "I was just minding my own

business, practicing my swing, when the wind shifted. It was an accident, really." He said to her with innocent, pleading eyes.

"You stay right here while I straighten this out," she said, as she followed the manager into the office.

Eric sat on the lobby bench nervously tapping his foot on the olive green linoleum. Christmas decorations blanketed the walls, while a light bulb flashed on and off overhead. Soon, a stream of elderly residents made their way slowly toward the dining room. They were all dressed in bright, holiday formal wear. They reminded Eric of the *Lawrence Welk* Christmas reruns his grandpa used to watch on television. Eric was probably the only kid in his school who knew the lyrics to "Chattanooga Choo Choo." He didn't dare admit it.

A large woman wearing a sparkly red sweater and flowing skirt led the group. Her wooden cane creaked as it supported her. A toothless man hurried behind her on a walker that clicked with every step. The black and white saddle shoes on his feet scooted across the floor with a swishing sound. Immediately behind him came an elegantly dressed woman in a wheelchair that squeaked like a nest of mice with every rotation of the wheels. The

340

MISTLETOE MADNESS

Santa hat on her head and the jingle bell suspended from the armrest reminded Eric of an elf. All of these sounds reverberated through the hall in an odd music-like rhythm. *Creak, Swoosh, Click, Jingle!* Eric half expected to hear an orchestra strike up and to see dancers appear.

"Geez! I feel like I'm in the Twilight Zone," Eric said to himself as he rolled his eyes.

"That was quite a hit, young man." Eric jumped, startled by the tall man wearing an old hat and dark sunglasses who appeared from behind him. The man was slightly slouched over and his aged bow tie sagged.

"Uh, thanks, I guess. I don't think they're too impressed, though," Eric said, motioning over his shoulder to his mother who was talking on the phone.

The old man didn't look, "Oh. Now breaking windows is just part of being a kid," the old man said with a raspy chuckle. The gentleman turned toward the dining hall as the smell of sweet potatoes and the sound of an out-of-tune piano wafted towards them.

"Ah, food, music, and baseball, my favorite things," he said with a smile. "It's too darned quiet around here during the holidays, though. I wish more kids would come to visit." Then he tipped his hat, and extended a long thin stick to the floor making wide, sweeping movements that tapped along the baseboards as he walked. Tap, Tap, Tap!

"He's blind," Eric whispered to himself, as he watched the old man disappear down the hall. How'd he know . . . Before he could finish his thought, his mother and Ms. Larsen returned.

"Well, Son, I've assured Ms. Larsen that you will be happy to pay the $75 repair bill," his mother said with an odd smile.

Eric shot straight up in shock. "I don't have $75 dollars! Mom, it was an accident."

"I know it was, Eric. But it's time you take responsibility for your actions, even when it's an accident. You can work off your debt tomorrow. Happy Trails has two employees out with the flu, so they need help in the kitchen."

"But Mom, tomorrow's the big game! You know how important it is. We've never played a winter tournament before." Eric protested.

"There will be other baseball games." She shook Ms. Larsen's hand and guided Eric toward the door just as the repairman arrived, puffs of snow trailing in behind him. Arguing would get Eric nowhere.

"This would have been the biggest game of my life but I'm doomed to spend my Saturday in the most un-cool place in town."

By eleven o'clock Saturday, Eric had mopped the floor, scrubbed greasy pots and pans, and found a lost set of false teeth, along with a lone jinglebell earring. The poinsettia wine glasses from the night before were still waiting to be washed. And the lunch crowd was due shortly. His own stomach grumbled like a hungry lion.

When Ms. Larsen told him he could take a break, Eric slumped into a red velvet chair near the dining room Christmas tree. He ate his ham and cheese sandwich, chips, and apple; then glanced at his watch with a sigh. He had practiced for this game for weeks and now his buddies played without him. He closed his eyes and imagined his team counting on him to break a tie for the playoffs. He felt his breathing slow and his muscles relax as his mind drifted into dreamland.

The crowd chanted his name. Eric! Eric! Eric! He stepped forward with his lucky bat and kicked the snow off home plate. The pitcher's stance indicated a fastball. Eric's heart raced. He gripped the bat, pulled it high over

MISTLETOE MADNESS

his right shoulder and challenged the ball coming toward him. He swung with all his might and let the bat fall to the ground as he began to run. The coach yelled something he couldn't quite hear; then a familiar sound . . . Crash!

"It was an accident," Eric shouted as he awoke with a start and jumped straight to his feet. Sweat streamed down his freckled face. The elderly diners stared at him and whispered to each other, then pointed to the blind man sitting at a table nearby. The man had knocked his glass off the table and it shattered as it hit the floor. Eric rubbed his eyes, took a deep breath, and hurried to the kitchen for a broom and dustpan.

"Strike two," the man said as he shook his head. "You didn't think you held the market on breaking glass, did you?" the man asked. "The name's Ben Thompson, young man," he extended a wrinkled hand in Eric's direction. Eric shook it awkwardly.

"Eric Matthews, Sir. Um, how'd you know it was me? I mean, since you're blind and all."

"Well now, who else would plead innocence over a silly old broken glass? There's no mistaking the sound of a wooden bat on cowhide or the nervous toe tapping of a kid waiting to 'pay the fiddler'." Eric had to smile. He liked this old man.

"I guess I kind of fell asleep. I always seem to be in the wrong place at the right time. My team's playing in the winter tournament right now and I'm missing it," Eric said as he set the dustpan down and plopped into the chair with a thud.

"I broke my share of windows playing baseball on these very same streets. My momma tanned my hide more than once," the man laughed at the memories. "Pretty soon my buddies and I had to find other ways to keep busy, so we formed a street band. We didn't have none of these high-fangled gadgets you have now. We gathered whatever we found in the alleys or what we could sneak from our kitchens. Yes sir, we were the coolest cats in town, playing jazz with trash can lids, spoons, glasses, soda bottles, and an old rusty harmonica. You name it, we could make it sing. It wasn't the same as playing a game of ball, but we sure had us a good time and made some folks smile." A wide grin spread across his face. His eyes disappeared beneath waves of wrinkles, but Eric thought he looked younger for a moment.

Eric's curiosity finally got the better of him. "So you haven't always been blind?"

"No. When I was about fifteen, I found myself in the right place at the wrong time," he took a long, deep sigh before continuing. "It was the first game of the season, 1931. I had the best seat in the park, just behind home plate. I could see the whites of the players' eyes. What I didn't see was the ball as it ripped off the bat. It nailed me right between the eyes and knocked me out cold. At least that's what they tell me." Eric was mesmerized by the tale.

"The poor fellow who popped that fly ball felt awfully bad. He showed up at the hospital with the game ball, autographed by the whole team. He even played me a little tune on his own harmonica," Mr. Thompson said.

"I don't play any instrument unless you count a trick my grandpa taught me with crystal wine glasses. And I can play "Old MacDonald" with my armpits, but Mom hates that." Mr. Thompson laughed as if he understood.

Eric noticed Ms. Larsen clear her throat and glare at him from the kitchen door. His break was over.

Mr. Thompson got up to return to his room, "Well, sounds like the warden's calling you. I hope we'll be seeing you for dinner tonight. The sounds of a young voice are music to my ears." Then he smiled, patted Eric on the shoulder, and made his way toward the hall.

The tapping of the walking stick soon joined the rhythmic clicking and squeaking of the returning walker, wheelchair, and cane. The *Lawrence Welk* crowd from the previous night was making their way toward the dining room, dressed in their finest, as usual.

Creak, Swoosh, Creak, Jingle!

Eric had a sudden thought. He wanted to do something nice for Mr. Thompson. Something that didn't have to be seen with his eyes. Something that wouldn't slip out of his hands. Something that would make him feel young again and make him smile, if only for a moment.

"Maybe this isn't the coolest place to be on a Saturday, but if I have to be here I'd might as well liven it up and make an old man smile. It is the Christmas season, after all. If Mr. Thompson thinks it's too quiet around here; then maybe everyone else does, too," Eric said aloud to himself as he stared at the wine glasses waiting for him. He was suddenly excited about washing and polishing. These old, mismatched glasses would soon be melody.

He rushed back to the dining room and met the familiar group just sitting at a table with their trays of food. Eric introduced himself politely; then, smiling ear to ear, he shared his idea. From a distance, Ms. Larsen watched curiously as Eric pointed from the wheelchair to the cane and then to the walker with its jingling bells. Each person, in turn, smiled and beamed with excitement. Everyone nodded and laughed. Eric rushed to get approval from Ms. Larsen and made a special phone call to his mother. He had a favor to ask her and it couldn't wait. Both women were surprisingly supportive. Eric rushed through his work and set to planning the surprise. Dinner time would be far from quiet.

At 6:30 p.m., the dining hall was filled with the aromas of a buffet feast and the chattering from tables of anxious people who had heard rumors of what was to come. For a while, Eric was afraid Mr. Thompson wouldn't be down for dinner. And then he heard the familiar tapping of his walking stick on the floor. That's when his cheeks began to redden.

"Hi, Mr. Thompson. I, um, saved your table for you," Eric said slyly as he directed the old man to his favorite table. He noticed that the old sagging bow tie had been replaced with a bolo tie, and a crumpled brown paper bag was tucked under his arm.

"Well, good evening Mr. Matthews. How nice of

you to join us." Then Mr. Thompson leaned toward Eric and spoke in a hushed voice, "Do you suppose they'll let you off easy for good behavior?" The two laughed like old friends.

"Maybe, but not yet. I mean, I have a surprise for you. Please wait right here." Eric rushed off to a table surrounded by the familiar faces of his new cohorts and whispered instructions. The room suddenly grew quiet.

"Ahem," Eric cleared his throat. "Mr. Thompson, I peeked out into the alley, raided the kitchen, and found some pretty 'cool cats' wandering these halls. My new friends and I have pulled together a street band right here at Happy Trails. You happen to be in the right place at the right time." Mr. Thompson looked confused and curious.

His mother walked through the door just as Eric picked up the walking stick, laid it on the table and placed the handle in Mr. Thompson's hand. "Mr. Thompson, you would do us a great favor if you would tap your stick on the table three times." He smiled brightly then added, "Oh, don't worry, I've moved all the glasses."

Mr. Thompson beamed and did as he was asked, *tap, tap, tap*. The off-tune piano began playing. Eric stood over the wine glasses, filled with varying levels of water, ran his wet fingers over the rims and listened to them sing, just as his grandpa had shown him over years of Christmas dinners. When the third measure began, Mr. Thompson pulled an old rusty harmonica out of his pocket and joined in. Soon, everyone danced from their chairs to the tune of "Chattanooga Choo Choo." From every table in the room, people joined the band. Some rattled spoons together while others jingled Christmas bells or added the rhythmic squeaking and clicking of walkers, wheelchairs, and canes. Still others added the soft clapping of kind, wrinkled hands.

Eric looked at Mr. Thompson, running the harmonica along his pursed lips with great precision. A single tear of joy fell to the old man's lap as seventy years melted from the moment. The sounds of youthful memories danced off walls and engulfed everyone in the room. Then Eric spotted his mother standing in the corner, swaying her hips and clapping to the music. She winked at him with a smile he hadn't seen in some time. The one that says, "you're the most amazing kid on earth." In that moment, Eric was as proud of himself as she was.

When the music stopped, the clapping, laughing, and chattering continued for some time. People sat a little taller and smiled a little wider. Eric shook Mr. Thompson's hand and strangers patted them both on the back.

"Well, I am speechless Eric, my boy. I'd say you've become the leader of the band. Thanks for letting me sit in," Mr. Thompson said.

"Merry Christmas, Mr. Thompson. You know, I've never had so much fun in my life. This is almost better than baseball. Almost."

"Oh, I nearly forgot," Mr. Thompson felt for the brown paper bag and handed it to Eric. "I don't have any grandkids so I'd like you to have this. Just a little Christmas gift. You can open it when you get home."

"Wow, thanks," Eric tried to ignore the lump in his throat as he stared at the crumpled bag. "I called my mom earlier and asked if I could invite a friend for Christmas. Would you like to spend the day with us?"

Mr. Thompson smiled as his eyes welled up with tears. He straightened up as much as possible and replied, "Food, music, baseball, and friends. My favorite things. I would like that very much."

Eric hugged the man, surprising even himself. Who knew it would make him feel so good just to make someone smile. The baseball game hadn't crossed his mind in hours.

Later that night, as Eric watched the snow from his bedroom window, he remembered the brown bag from Mr. Thompson. As he opened it, the sight of the aged bow tie made him smile. It was wrapped around a very old, withered baseball glove. "Cool," he said. As he unfolded the glove, a slightly yellowed baseball rolled onto his bed. It was dated 1931 and had been autographed by Babe Ruth and the New York Yankees. Eric was stunned. For hours he lay there staring at it until exhaustion and a strange sense of calm lulled him to sleep. The last thought he remembered was that this was the coolest Saturday he had ever spent. He couldn't wait for Christmas Day.

As he drifted off to sleep, a heavy fog filled his dreams. A crowd called his name; the sounds of excited feet rumbled through the stands. While he cleared the dirt and snow from home plate, an odd clicking and squeaking could be heard in the distance. This was the moment he had been waiting for. He gripped the bat and eyed the baseball. Looking back, Eric saw a tall figure of a legend over one shoulder and the sight of Babe Ruth over the other. And, in the background, a street band played

MISTLETOE MADNESS

"Chattanooga Choo Choo" for the leader of the band.

Donna Bowman Bratton

Day After Chirstmas

Day after Christmas
and all through the house,
the dogs were sacked out
and so was the mouse.

Stockings were empty.
The chimney was bare.
Dad was indulging
in post-Christmas fare.

The children were out
shopping the malls,
spending their money
from the in-laws.

MISTLETOE MADNESS

Mom did the dishes
and wondered with fear,
"Who'll help me take down
decorations this year?"

With New Years coming
and Christmas so near,
I wish you patience
and Holiday Cheer!

Elizabeth O. Dulemba

355

MISTLETOE MADNESS

Merry Christmas

Terri L. Sanders

Illustration By Terri L. Sanders

356

CONTRIBUTORS

The wonderful stories, poems and artwork in this book were submitted by the authors and illustrators listed below. We are truly grateful they took the time to share their talent with us. Take a moment to get to know these amazing people!

Jessica Anderson's passion is writing literature for children. She's had short story and craft article acceptances for such magazines as *Highlights for Children* and *Wee Ones Magazine*. Jessica's middle grade and young adult novels are currently under consideration. She is a member of SCBWI and will graduate October 2004 from Hollins University with a Master of Arts in Children's Literature. Recently, she won the Shirley Henn Memorial Award for a young adult novel in progress. When not writing, Jessica likes to travel and spend time with family and friends. She lives in Austin, Texas with her husband Michael and her dog Buster, a Yorkshire "Terror."

Dorothy Baughman lives in Eclectic, Alabama and has been happily married for 44 years. She has three children and four grandchildren. She has worked in many different fields including telephone operator, EKG Technician, Veterinary assistant and she is a former editor of the Eclectic Observer.

Dorothy has been a Freelance writer for over 30 years and has the following publishing credits: *Pineys Summer*, published by Coward, McCann & Geoghegan. Reprint *Pineys Summer*, *Mystery Of Lost Creek*, *Secret Of Connelly Castle* and *Who Wants To Be A Lady Anyway?*, all by New Age Dimensions ebook 2004. These four books are being combined into one volume and will be out

CONTRIBUTORS

soon in print called *The Dorothy Baughman Collection.*
Her Children's Magazines credits include: *Red Cross Youth News, Junior Discoveries, David Cook take home paper, The Friend, The Vine, Highlights For Children, Highlights Anthology, My Friend* plays and *Mistletoe Madness* Children's Anthology 2004.
She has also published four adult mysteries and stories in 28 adult magazines.

Donna Bowman Bratton has always dreamed in words. As a child, Donna tucked notebooks into her blue-jean waistbands as she cantered her horse across the family ranch toward her secret refuge. The outstretched limb of a giant oak tree welcomed the weight of her words as they churned dramatically within her imagination and spilled onto the pages of notebooks as poems, stories, plays and diaries. Dreams always made it to paper.
There was plenty of material for a young girl with a vivid imagination and a love of books. Youth was spent in horseshow arenas where competition was fierce. In addition to the Quarter horses her family raised, Donna enjoyed a childhood filled with wide open spaces and plenty of animals. Dogs, cats, chickens, ducks, cows, guineas and even a pet skunk named "Stinky" became characters in early tall tales.
For fifteen years Donna enjoyed a successful insurance career but never lost the yearning to share stories. Though her wide open spaces are now surrounded by homes and the giant oak tree no longer awaits her, Donna can still be found spinning tales late into the night while her husband and two children wander through their own dreamlands in the refuge of her home in Round Rock, Texas. In addition to children's fiction and non-fiction, Donna has written plays and skits for local audiences and has been a frequent

CONTRIBUTORS

contributor to local newspapers. Ms. Bratton is a member of SCBWI and a graduate of the Institute of Children's Literature."
Look for Donna Bowman Bratton's articles, short stories and upcoming novel. Ms. Bratton can be contacted at dbratton3@austin.rr.com

Leslie Carmichael lives in Calgary, Alberta, Canada with her husband, three children and two cats. This is her first published children's story. She likes to travel and has been to exciting places like Europe, Egypt and Taiwan. She also loves to read, sing, make costumes, study everything about the Middle Ages, and especially, write! Her work has been published in American Miniaturist (she likes dollhouses, too), *The Canadian Quilter and Storyteller*: Canada's Short Story Magazine.

Karen A. Carpenter Few writers love to write about holidays more than Karen Ann Carpenter. She has written dozens of stories for children; many of them take place at Christmas time. Karen also writes a column entitled: *Celebrate The Now*, where she combines her passion for holidays with her love of cooking. This column relates the history and meaning of holidays from all over the world, and includes an appropriate recipe for every holiday.
Karen is also fascinated with the supernatural. She writes dark and spooky fiction for adults, as well as nonfiction articles about life's uncanny mysteries. For information about Karen's free holiday newsletter visit: *CelebrateTheNow.com* or write to Karen at: KarenAnnCarpenter@yahoo.com.

Mary Cronin wrote her very first poem when she was in first grade. It was about the tooth fairy. The principal claimed to like it so much that she put it in the safe in her office. Mary wonders if it

CONTRIBUTORS

is still there. Mary, who lives on Cape Cod with her partner and daughter, divides her time between teaching and writing poetry. She writes her best poetry when her Wheaten Terrier, Oona, is curled up next to her. Mary collects Christmas music from around the world: her current favorites are from Ireland and Jamaica. Mary hopes to one day travel around the world with her family, meeting lots of fun people and collecting some more Christmas tunes. She can be reached at maryecronin@yahoo.com.

Lucia De León is a 17 year old singer, actress, song writer, and poet. She wrote her first song at the age of 12 and is actively pursuing a career as a singer and song writer. She lives in Marshall, Texas with her mother.

Elizabeth O. Dulemba lives in the beautiful North Georgia Mountains, a little east of nowhere. She and her husband share their home with a big yellow dog, a raucous puppy, and a tiny cat who rules them all.

After a lifetime of art training, Elizabeth majored in Graphic Design at the University of Georgia. During her fifteen years in the Graphics Arts, most of her career revolved around creating for children, such as for a clothing line, several candy companies, and an animated laser show. She was always in-house illustrator, even during her roles as Art Director. If you could wear it, buy it, enjoy it or be informed by it, she could create it.

A few years ago, Elizabeth jumped off the corporate merry-go-round to focus on writing and illustrating for children. She now contributes regularly to children's and trade magazines, and is working on several picture books. You can learn more about Elizabeth at her web site: http://dulemba.com.

360

CONTRIBUTORS

Rusty Fischer lives in Orlando, Florida and writes full-time. He is the author of the previous Christmas titles *O Tannenbaum: The Story of the Last Christmas Tree* (PublishAmerica, 2004) and *Project Angel Tree: A Christmas Miracle* (iUniverse, 2003).

Ardeen Fredrick, creator of Joshua and the Innkeeper, and her husband Jim, celebrated their fiftieth wedding anniversary last May. Over 100 people signed the guest book, the same book that was used at their wedding reception.

The working title was Joshua's Ewe. In working with that title she pledged that any profit that would be realized would be sent to Heifer Project to provide lambs for children in third world countries.

No such promise was appropriate for Innkeepers, so she pledges now that any profit generated by either short story will be sent to Heifer Project.

The final title was *Joshua Was There: A Shepherd's Guide to the Holy Night*. Of the first three pieces of writing she submitted for publication, three were accepted. To date, out of six submissions, she has had three acceptances.

Barbara Hollace, this is your life. We all wish for our fifteen minutes of fame, but once it arrives we are at a loss for words. Her earliest attempts at writing were homemade greeting cards.

Her expertise moved up a notch and she began seriously writing poetry at the age of fourteen. She self published a book of her poetry, and it had a short run. Through her years of university and post-graduate work, her creative writing was directed mostly to school assignments and not wanderings of the heart and mind.

The last five years have seen a revival in her writing interests. She currently writes a monthly article for the *CommuniQué*, a newsletter directed at the low-income audience in her community. Her repertoire includes newsletters, inspirational pieces, poetry, greeting cards and children's stories. Currently, she is exploring several non-fiction ideas, but she has the most fun writing stories for children.

As a child, reading was one of her favorite pastimes. She is proud to be a part of this short story collection and to give children a wonderful book to enjoy for many years. If you have any comments or information about other writing opportunities, please contact her at hollacewritingservices@yahoo.com.

One closing tidbit: She never did master the art of roller skating as a child, so she thinks roller blades are definitely out as an adult sports option.

Lois Miner Huey is a historical archeologist working for the State of New York. She writes non-fiction for kids magazines. This is her first fiction piece and is based on her own experiences as a kid playing the chimes at 6:00 each night at the local Methodist church.

Valerie Hunter is a secondary English education major at The College of New Jersey. Her stories have been accepted in children's magazines, including *Cricket* and *The Sunville Spotlight*. Valerie first created the characters of Emily and Zane when she was in middle school, but "A Gift for Zane" is the first time they saw print.

Carla Joinson spent ten years in St. Louis, Missouri but "grew up" in the small town of West Frankfort, Illinois amid the coal

CONTRIBUTORS

mining region which later became the background for her young adult novel *A Diamond in the Dust*. Carla attended Southern Illinois University and received a Bachelor of Science degree in Food and Nutrition. A member of ROTC, she was also commissioned a second lieutenant at this time, and moved to Ellsworth AFB, South Dakota, where she was a Food Service Officer and later an Operations Officer in the 44th Services Squadron. After leaving the Air Force, Carla worked as an administration supervisor until she began her free-lance career.

Carla has published more than 200 nonfiction articles in magazines like *First for Women, Parenting, HR Magazine,* and *Employment Management Today*, as well as in publications like *Highlights for Children, Faces* and *Calliope*. She also presents workshops and teaches numerous continuing education courses on writing.

Carla has published two young adult novels, *March of Glory* (1994) by Royal Fireworks Press, and *A Diamond in the Dust* (2001) by Dial Books for Young Readers. She is available for school visits and author appearances and can be contacted through her web site at www.carlajoinson.com.

Catherine Jones' oldest son, David, wanted to design tennis shoes for Nike when he grew up! She has used his interesting exploits in several of her published stories. A member of the Society of Children's Book Writers and Illustrators, Catherine has been a published author since 1993 with stories and articles appearing in *Highlights for Children, Cobblestone, Jack and Jill, Hopscotch, Boys' Quest,* and other magazines. She has also published two books for children. When she is not writing, she teaches music, creative writing, and Shakespeare to children of all

CONTRIBUTORS

ages. She is married, has two sons and lives in the beautiful Texas Hill Country.

Regina Kubelka is a published illustrator working in various mediums such as watercolor, pencil and digital mixed media. She has a Bachelor of Fine Art in Illustration from Rocky Mountain College of Art & Design in Denver and also completed studies in Commercial Art & Advertising at Texas State Technical College.

Her work has appeared in several publications and countless commercial designs. Most recently, Regina was selected to be a featured artist to be represented on the stock illustration website, www.theSpiritSource.com where she showcases 16 images based on social and spiritual themes.

Currently Regina resides in Austin, Texas where she successfully operates "Illustration Central", her own advertising design firm specializing in illustration. Regina also pursues a love for writing and illustrating for the children's market.

You can check out more of Regina's work by going to her website at www.illustrationcentral.com.

Kay Ann LaLone lives with her husband, Dan, and her three sons Daniel, David and Christopher. She has written several short stories and is currently working on a middle grade novel and a young adult novel. In addition to her writing, she sells on ebay, home schools her youngest son and plans on opening a bait shop with her husband. She will gladly answer your letters at lalone1@juno.com or snail mail: Kay Ann LaLone, 217 N. 8th St., Lansing, MI 48912.

Joanne Linden is a former elementary school teacher who spends a good share of her time writing. She is the mother of three

364

CONTRIBUTORS

children and grandmother of Emilie. She lives in a wooded area in Wisconsin with her husband and their Scottish Terrier. Reading, art, writing, and "hanging out at our lake cottage" is what she likes to do best. Even in snowy blowy winter!

Her publishing credits include: *Juniper Creek Press* (2002), a literacy publication, *Grit Family Magazine* (2003), *Wee Ones E-Magazine* (2004), *Parents and Children Together Online* (2004), a literacy site, *Blooming Tree Press* (2004), a Christmas Story Anthology, *Crinkles Magazine* (2003), (2004) She writes on assignment for this publication, *Think and Discover* (2004).

Tricia Mathison was born and raised in Texas. She can only remember seeing snow once growing up. Today, she lives in Florida (where it still doesn't snow) with her husband, Keith, and her two children, Sarah and Joseph. Her daughter's strong desire to have snow for Christmas was the inspiration for "Winter Wonderland". Tricia has written stories, poems and articles for a variety of children's magazines, including *Highlights for Children* and *Wee Ones*.

Susan Meyers is an Oklahoma author who resides with her husband, son and one spoiled cat. She's the author of several published short stories. You can learn more about Susan at her website, http://members.cox.net/sameyers/Children.html

Paula Miller is a homeschooling mom to three sons and an aspiring novelist for both women and children's fiction. She has several articles in family e-zines such as *Mommy Tales* (2004), *Christian Mommies* (2004), *Sarah's Seed* (2004) and *A Mom's Love* (2004). She and her family make their home in the Midwest. You can visit her at www.geocities.com/paulamiller_writer for

CONTRIBUTORS

samples of her articles and excerpts from her longer novels.

L.C. Mohr has been a contributing editor to several publications and has written fiction and non-fiction for the Internet and numerous print publications throughout the country. Her nine grandchildren are a constant, though noisy source of inspiration. She is a member of Mystery Writers of America and the International Women's Writing Guild.

Deborah M. Nigro, a native Bostonian, has authored several books for family reading, including 'John F. Kennedy: The Promise of Camelot'(amazon.com), which was approved for sale by the U. S. National Park Service. Her work has appeared nationally in *First for Women, Highlights for Children*, the Macfadden Group magazines and many other publications. "Two Kinds of Christmas" was inspired by Deborah's holiday season visit to New Zealand, where she discovered her own 'Christmas in the sun.' Contact Deborah at: debmon2002@yahoo.com.

Carol J. Rhodes' widely published work includes essays, poetry, short stories, non-fiction, and plays. It has been featured in *Country Home, Good Old Boat*, and Texas magazines; *Houston Chronicle, Stroud (England) News and Journal*, and *Christian Science Monitor* newspapers; as well as journals *New Texas 2001; RE:AL, Sojourn*, and numerous anthologies. She received the Word is Art award from Texas Writer's League for her non-fiction article, "It's 9 AM . . . Do You Know Where Your Desk Is?" In addition, one of her plays was produced for an off-Broadway summer festival.

Carol teaches business writing for the Small Business

Development Center of the University of Houston, her alma mater, and creative writing at The Women's Institute. Married forty-one years, she has three children, four cats and three dogs. Some of her work may be viewed at www.caroljrhodes.com, or reach her at cjrhodes@houston.rr.com.

Velia Rolff was born in Colon, Republic of Panama. She owes her creativity to her father, Mr. David Martinez, who was a dedicated pharmacist and a very creative man.

After school, when she helped her father in his pharmacy, he would give her a nickel that she would take to the corner store that sold little fairy tales booklets. Years later, her parents sent her to the Pan American Institute in Panama City, where she learned English and had her poems published in the yearbook. After graduation she worked in an American company, married an American, Mr. Marvin Rolff and came to the United States. She attended the University of Texas at Austin and took courses on Creative Writing at Austin Community College. She has also received a certificate from the Institute of Children's Literature.

After her husband passed away, she became an American citizen and worked as a bilingual secretary until she retired. She has joined the Writers' League of Texas and has the following publishing credits: Her poems published in Spanish in Panama, an article in English in the Science of Mind Magazine, and her short story in Mistletoe Madness. Currently she enjoys writing, cartooning and lives in Austin, Texas with her two children and three grandchildren.

Christine Gerber Rutt Christmas always begins one week early for Christine. The presents aren't under the Christmas tree yet

but there is a table filled with food and friends to celebrate her birthday. Christine was born in the United States but now currently lives in Switzerland. She works as a writer, translator and mother. She writes regularly for the *Basel Childbirth Trust* and *Hello Basel*. She has also organized/founded a critique group in Switzerland of writers for children. She has translated for various agencies from art museums to sport associations to the newspaper but, most of all more than anything, she likes eating pistachio ice cream while walking along the Rhine River with her daughter.
She can be contacted at gerberrutt@freesurf.ch.

Terri L. Sanders as an artist, Terri has experience with logo design, oil painting, and cartooning. She has coupled her love for art with writing for children. "Rainbow Spider" and "Night Flies" are her fully illustrated ebooks. Other projects are: illustrations for puzzles and a picture book, short stories for *Essential Skills*, and two Christian clipart cds. Terri resides with her husband, Terry and three sons in Irvington, IL. Visit her website at www.sanderst.com/terri.html.Email:sanderst@netwitz.net

Gloria Singendonk spends an inordinate amount of time researching and writing historical fiction and non-fiction. Her previous publications include several Canadian history articles in *FACES* magazine. She lives in Calgary, Alberta, Canada with her husband and three sons.

Linda Joy Singleton plots involve twins, cheerleaders, ghosts, psychics and clones. Linda Joy Singleton has published over 25 midgrade and YA books.
Her REGENERATION series from Berkley Books was chosen by the ALA as a 2001 Quick Pick Choice for reluctant young adult

CONTRIBUTORS

readers. It was also released in foreign and large-print editions, plus it was optioned by Fox for a year. And TWIN AGAIN, the first book in the series, MY SISTER THE GHOST, won the Eppie Award for the best children's book in 2003.

Linda has two new magical, mysterious series starting in Fall 2004:

STRANGE ENCOUNTERS #1. OH, NO! UFO! - 11 year old Cassie who has out of this world adventures on family trips.

THE SEER #1. DON'T DIE, DRAGONFLY - Sabine Rose is a teen detective with a 6th sense for solving mysteries.

When she's not writing, she enjoys life in the country with a barnyard of animals including horses, cats, dogs and pigs. She especially loves to hear from readers and speaking at schools and libraries. She collects vintage series books like Nancy Drew, Trixie Belden and Judy Bolton. Linda wrote The Stalking Snowman as a fun tribute to a Judy Bolton book she co-wrote with Margaret Sutton titled The Talking Snowman. See her website for more information: www.LindaJoySingleton.com.

When Linda is asked why she'd rather write for kids than adults, she says, "I love seeing the world through the heart of a child, where magic is real and every day begins a new adventure. I hope to inspire them to reach for their dreams. Writing for kids is a gift, a responsibility, and an honor."

Nanette Thorsen-Snipes lives in northeast Georgia and has been married to Jim for 28 years. She is the mother of four grown children and has three grandchildren, three granddogs, numerous grandkitties and one grandbird. Possum is her furry child, and the only one left at home. He also caught a bat in the basement and brought it upstairs as a "love" gift to her!

369

CONTRIBUTORS

The characters in the Great Christmas Tree Caper came from her unpublished book, The Great Gumshoe Caper. The book introduces six slap-happy characters including Gumshoe, the detective; Pris, his germ-free sister; Professor Backwards, who is true to his name; Germaine, who tries to keep everyone in line; Flapjack, the notorious loveable mutt, and Gabby, the cat with huge yellow-moon eyes and "attitude."

Nanette has been writing more than 20 years and has published over 500 articles, columns, devotions, stories, work-for-hire, and reprints in more than 50 publications including *Woman's World*, *The Lookout*, *Focus on the Family's Breakaway*, *Clubhouse* and *Clubhouse, Jr.*, among others. She has published numerous stories in more than 25 compilation books such as *Chicken Soup for the Christian Family Soul* and the *Christian Woman's Soul*, *God's Way* series, *God's Abundance*, *Stories for a Faithful Heart* and *Teen's Heart*, among others.

She has also written a work-for-hire children's book for Concordia Publishing; one chapter of stories in *Angels Where You Least Expect Them,* Publications International, Ltd.; several stories in *Grandmother and Mother Stories to Warm Your Heart*, Publications International, Ltd.; and 40 devotions in Honor Books' *Through the Night with God* and In *the Kitchen with God*, among others. Visit her Web site at www.nanettesnipes.com or contact her at nsnipes@bellsouth.net.

Marcia Strykowski lives in Bradford, Massachusetts, with her husband and their two children. She graduated from Northeastern University with a Bachelor's degree in Fine Arts and worked in publishing for ten years. Her stories, poems, and illustrations have appeared in many magazines and newspapers.

CONTRIBUTORS

Marion Tickner Marion Tickner grew up on a chicken farm during the Great Depression, so she is well acquainted with those printed feedbags. Because her mother didn't sew, she never had to wear a "sackcloth" dress to school. You can see samples of those feedbags at www.fabrics.net/joan301.asp.

Did you notice what happened to Elizabeth Johnson ("My Special Part") in last year's Christmas program? That actually happened to Marion. How embarrassing.

Marion claims to be too young to be a great-grandmother, but two adorable little girls call her Great-grandma Marion.

Marion is a graduate of Nyack College and The Institute of Children's Literature. Her experiences from working with children in church-related activities for many years have been her inspiration for writing for children's magazines. Marion Tickner, 200 Westfall Drive, Syracuse, NY, 13219

Charles Trevino enjoys writing for all ages. He resides in Spring, Texas with his wonderful wife and four fabulous children.

Deep in his heart is Texas and celebrating Christmas. "Carving out a Christmas" ran around in his mind while he was living on Galveston Bay, near the refineries. He is grateful to his teacher, Michael McFarland, for encouraging it to emerge as a short story from a homework assignment, and also to SCBWI for its professionalism, camaraderie, and weekly critique meetings.

Writing is the discipline. Reading is the feast. *Bon appetite.*

Luise van Keuren has written in various genres for young audiences, including poetry, stories, puppet plays, and full-length plays. Historical resources often provide her inspiration, as is the case with "The Remarkable Christmas Package." Among her

371

CONTRIBUTORS

credits is a historical play commissioned by the state of Vermont for its bicentennial, which toured every county in Vermont in an Equity production. Her story "Highland Gray," based on the life of an actual race horse, appeared in *Vermont Life* and received the Ralph Nading Hill Prize, given in honor of the New England historian. She is the author of poetry for "grown ups," which has appeared in *Sow's Ear Poetry* Review, *Blueline, Mindprints, Avocet, Connecticut Quarterly,* and other journals. She has also written about children in historical America in such works as *Rituals of Childhood* (University of Wisconsin Press, 2005) and *Girlhood in America* (ABC-CLIO Books, 2001). Luise van Keuren is a member of the English faculty of California University of Pennsylvania, near Pittsburgh.

Cassandra Reigel Whetstone lives in Northern California with her husband, two children, and two dogs. She began writing at age five, and hasn't stopped since. Look for her stories and poems in children's magazines such as *Ladybug* and *Highlights for Children.*
Although she has helped her own mother prepare a turkey dinner many times, she has never actually done it herself. While doing the research for "First Turkey," Cassandra considered cooking her first turkey dinner, but she chickened out.

Eugina White has traveled around the world before settling down with her husband and their German shepherd in a small town of Northern Massachusetts. After living in noisy and busy cities, she adores her peaceful and quiet neighborhood with fragrant flowers blooming all spring and summer long. Her favorite holiday is Christmas, as there is nothing better than sharing your happiness

CONTRIBUTORS

and gift giving.

Her experiences from teaching middle grades have been her inspiration for her writing. Among her credits are school curriculums and articles. Currently she is working on a fantasy novel. If you would like to contact her, please write to euginaw@hotmail.com.

Agy Wilson was born with a pencil and brush in her hand. She attended Portland School of Art, and later studied calligraphy with Bonnie Spiegel, Peter Halliday, Ieaun Rees and Paul Maurer. She's worked as a freelance calligrapher/graphic artist/crafts & calligraphy teacher, for almost twenty-five years. She's chased wax in Bronze founderies and painted ostrich eggs for Bush Gardens, Tampa Bay and key-opped in graphic reproduction facilities. After all kinds of jobs to contribute to her know-it-all attitude she'd finally decided to follow her true dream of writing and illustrating for children. Agy's founded two successful professional groups the former Calligraphers of Maine and Yellapalooza (www.yellapalooza.com), a critique group exclusively for people who both write and illustrate for children. Other credits include The Girl Who Helped the Puma, English Version for Shinseken Press; article and illustration for Children's Writers' and Illustrators' Markets 2004; article and illustration for Wee Ones on-line magazine, republished through SIRS. She now lives in Windham, Maine with her husband, two daughters and a passel of pets.